SUPER
RABBIT BOY
WORLD!

FUNSTON 64

SUPER
RABBIT BOY
WORLD

READ MORE PRESS START! BOOKS!

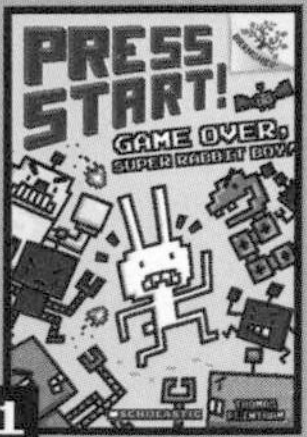
PRESS START!
GAME OVER, SUPER RABBIT BOY!
SCHOLASTIC
1

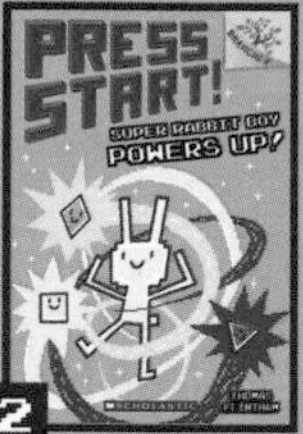
PRESS START!
SUPER RABBIT BOY POWERS UP!
SCHOLASTIC
THOMAS FLINTHAM
2

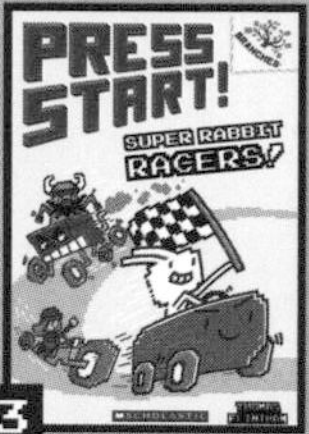
PRESS START!
SUPER RABBIT RACERS!
SCHOLASTIC
THOMAS FLINTHAM
3

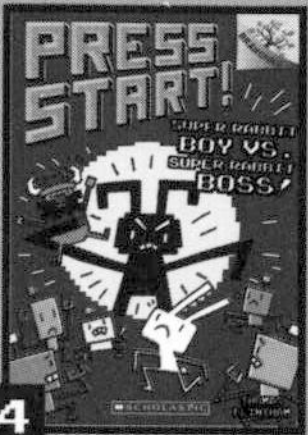
PRESS START!
SUPER RABBIT BOY VS. SUPER RABBIT BOSS!
SCHOLASTIC
THOMAS FLINTHAM
4

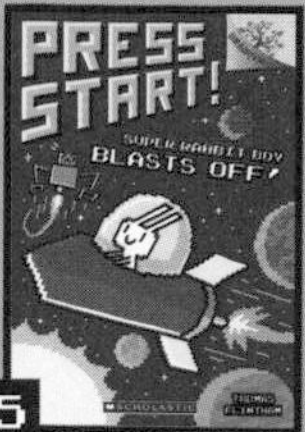
PRESS START!
SUPER RABBIT BOY BLASTS OFF!
SCHOLASTIC
THOMAS FLINTHAM
5

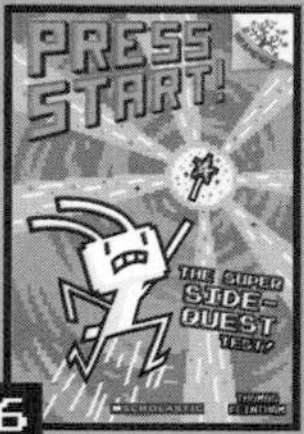
PRESS START!
THE SUPER SIDE-QUEST TEST!
SCHOLASTIC
THOMAS FLINTHAM
6

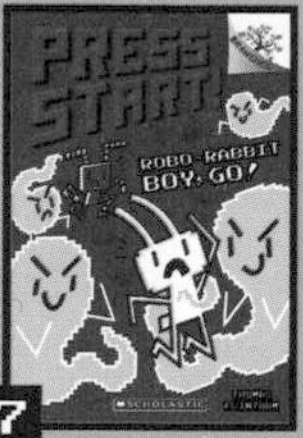
PRESS START!
ROBO-RABBIT BOY, GO!
SCHOLASTIC
7

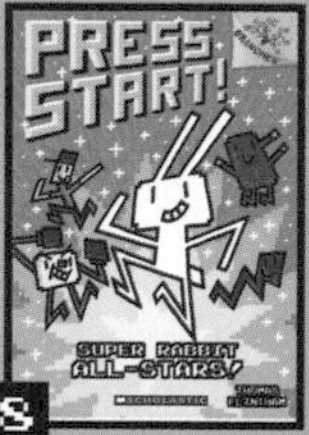
PRESS START!
SUPER RABBIT ALL-STARS!
SCHOLASTIC
THOMAS FLINTHAM
8

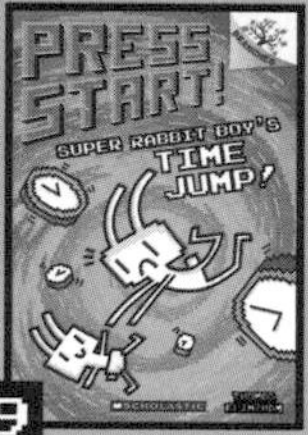
PRESS START!
SUPER RABBIT BOY'S TIME JUMP!
SCHOLASTIC
THOMAS FLINTHAM
9

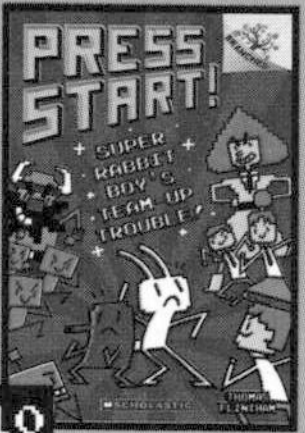
PRESS START!
SUPER RABBIT BOY'S TEAM-UP TROUBLE!
SCHOLASTIC
THOMAS FLINTHAM
10

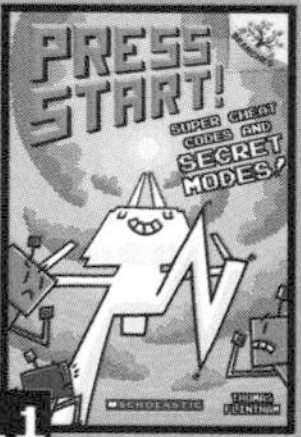
PRESS START!
SUPER CHEAT CODES AND SECRET MODES!
SCHOLASTIC
THOMAS FLINTHAM
11

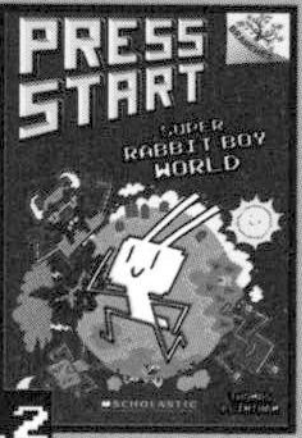
PRESS START
SUPER RABBIT BOY WORLD
SCHOLASTIC
THOMAS FLINTHAM
12

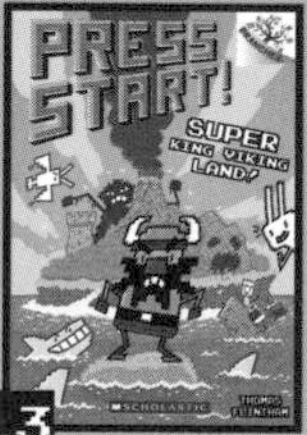
PRESS START!
SUPER KING VIKING LAND!
SCHOLASTIC
THOMAS FLINTHAM
13

MORE BOOKS COMING SOON!

PRESS START!

SUPER RABBIT BOY WORLD!

THOMAS FLINTHAM

BRANCHES

SCHOLASTIC INC.

FOR VINCENT

Copyright © 2022 by Thomas Flintham

All rights reserved. Published by Scholastic Inc., *Publishers since 1920.* SCHOLASTIC, BRANCHES, and associated logos are trademarks and/or registered trademarks of Scholastic Inc.

The publisher does not have any control over and does not assume any responsibility for author or third-party websites or their content.

No part of this publication may be reproduced, stored in a retrieval system, or transmitted in any form or by any means, electronic, mechanical, photocopying, recording, or otherwise, without written permission of the publisher. For information regarding permission, write to Scholastic Inc., Attention: Permissions Department, 557 Broadway, New York, NY 10012.

This book is a work of fiction. Names, characters, places, and incidents are either the product of the author's imagination or are used fictitiously, and any resemblance to actual persons, living or dead, business establishments, events, or locales is entirely coincidental.

Library of Congress Cataloging-in-Publication Data

Names: Flintham, Thomas, author, illustrator.
Title: Super Rabbit Boy World! / Thomas Flintham.
Description: First edition. | New York : Scholastic Inc., 2022. |
Series: Press start! ; 12 | Audience: Ages 5–7 | Audience: Grades K–2 |
Summary: King Viking is doing a lot of evil plans at the same time so,
with the help of Moon Girl and others, Super Rabbit Boy comes up
with a plan to stop the supervillain's attacks.
Identifiers: LCCN 2021034825 | ISBN 9781338569056 (paperback) |
ISBN 9781338569063 (library binding) |
Subjects: CYAC: Superheroes—Fiction. | Supervillains—Fiction. | Animals—Fiction.
Classification: LCC PZ7.1.F585 Svb 2022 | DDC [Fic]—dc23
LC record available at https://lccn.loc.gov/2021034825

10 9 8 7 6 5 4 3 2 1   22 23 24 25 26

Printed in China   62
First edition, September 2022
Edited by Katie Carella and Alli Brydon
Book design by Sarah Dvojack

TABLE OF CONTENTS

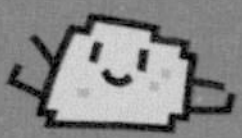

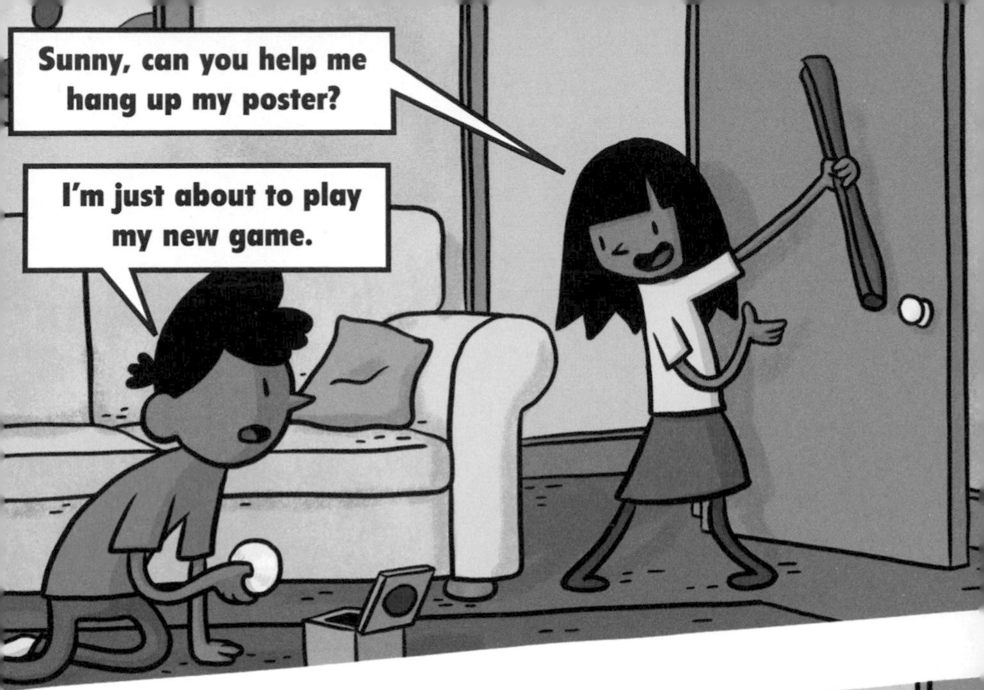
Sunny, can you help me hang up my poster?
I'm just about to play my new game.

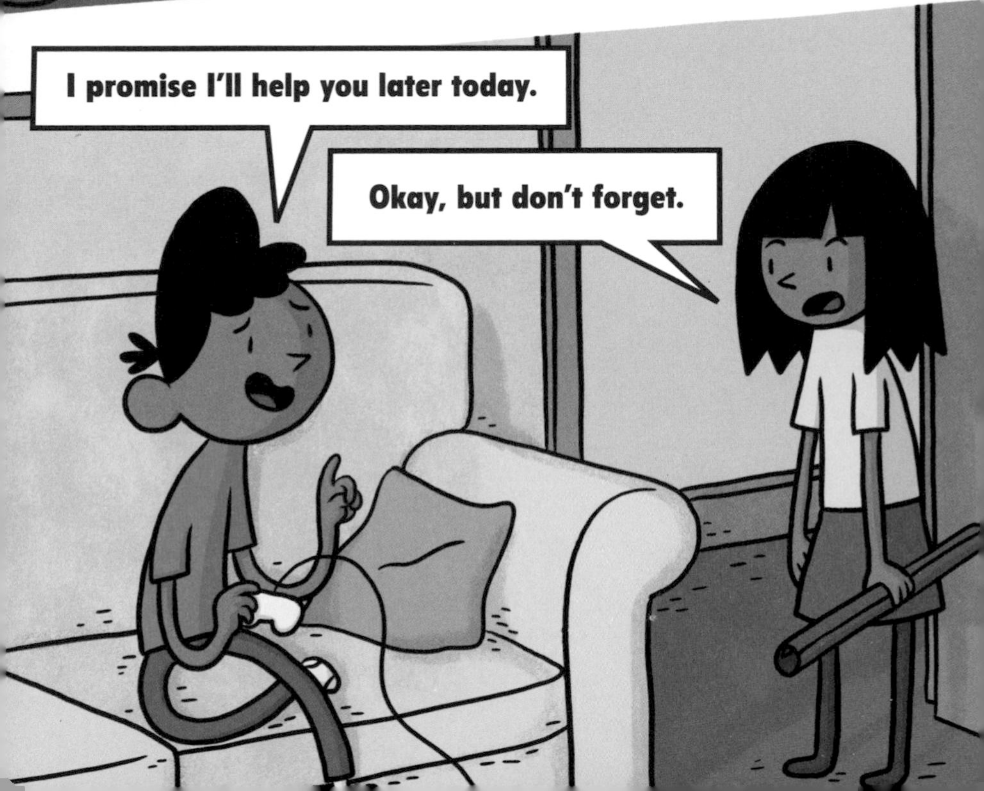
I promise I'll help you later today.
Okay, but don't forget.

1 PRESS START!

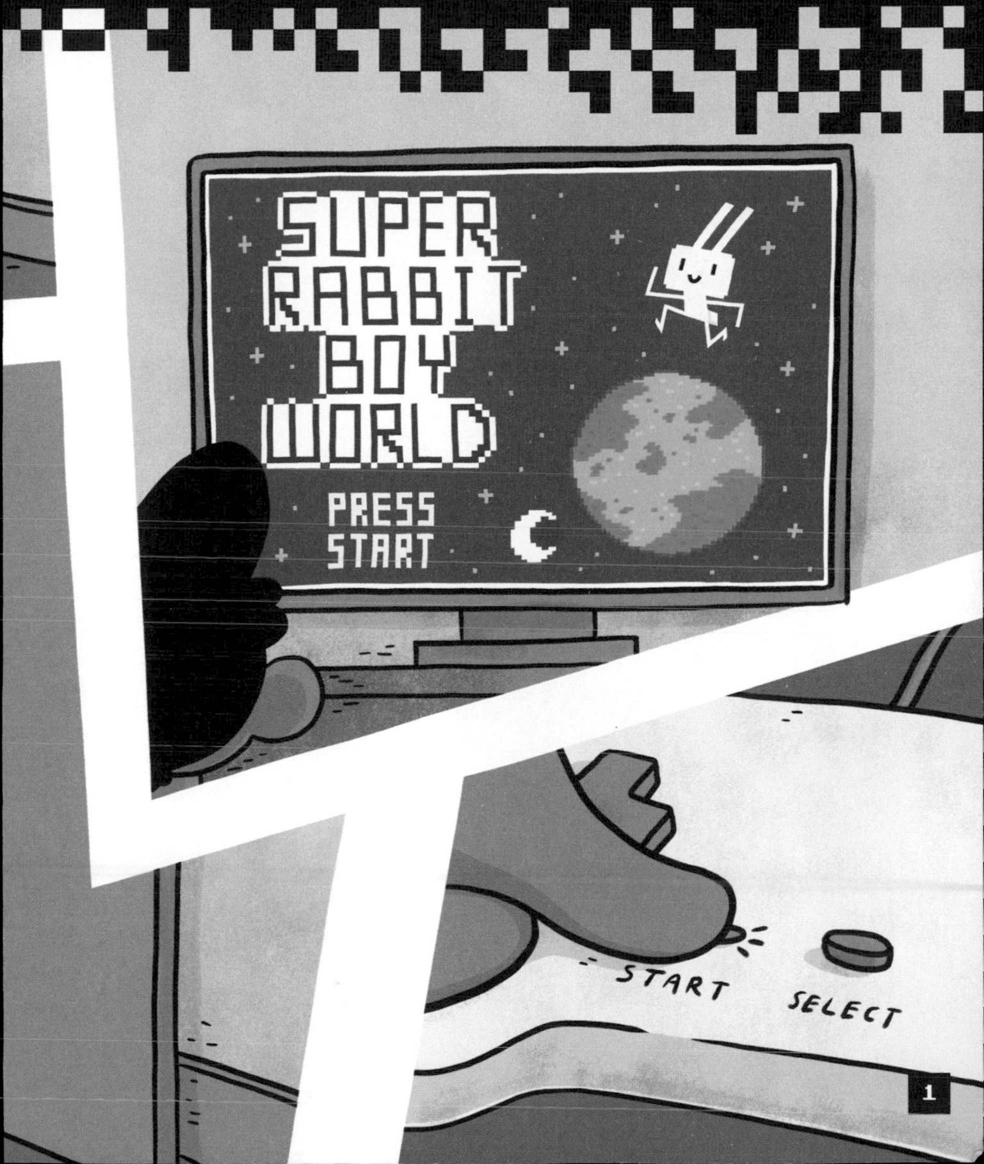
SUPER RABBIT BOY WORLD
PRESS START
START
SELECT

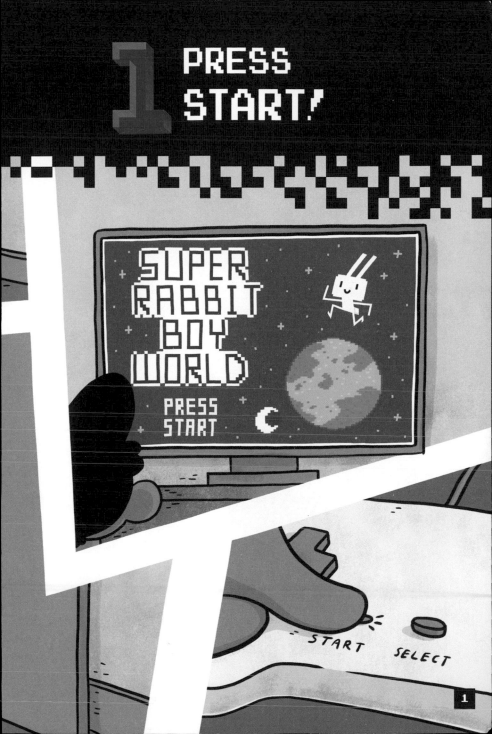

Super Rabbit Boy is visiting Moon Girl. She lives on the moon.

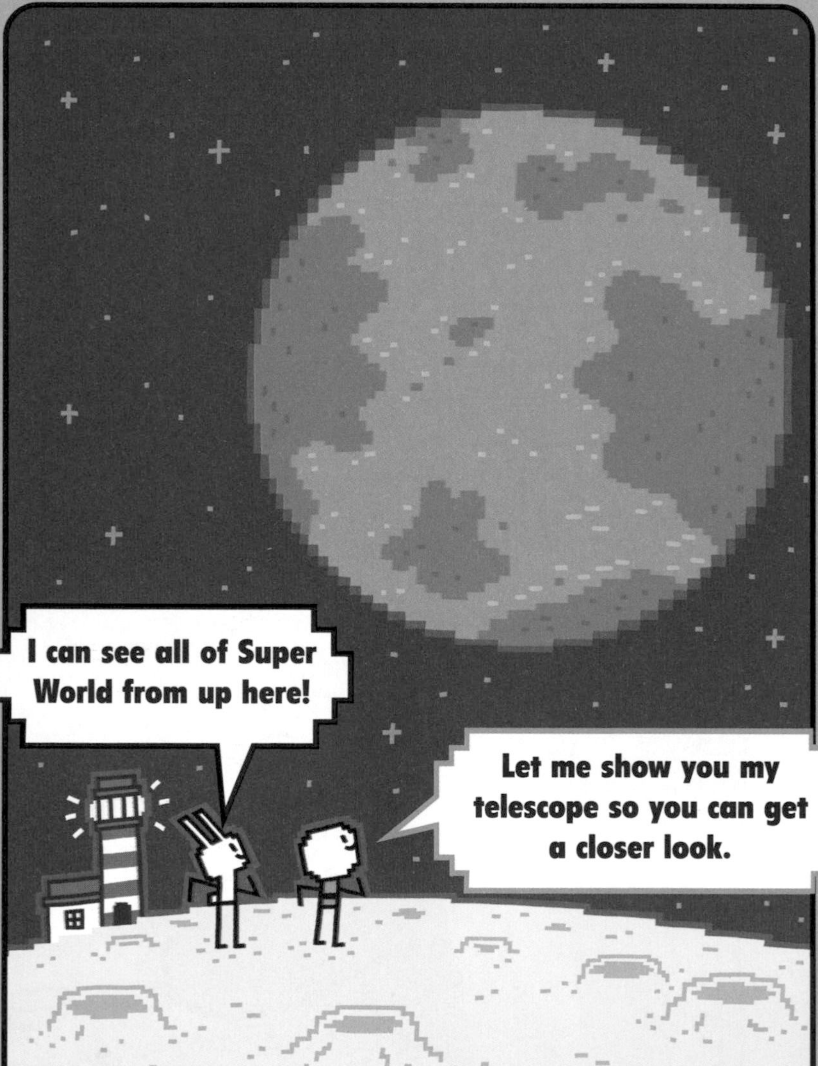
I can see all of Super World from up here!
Let me show you my telescope so you can get a closer look.

Moon Girl takes Super Rabbit Boy to her telescope. It's gigantic!

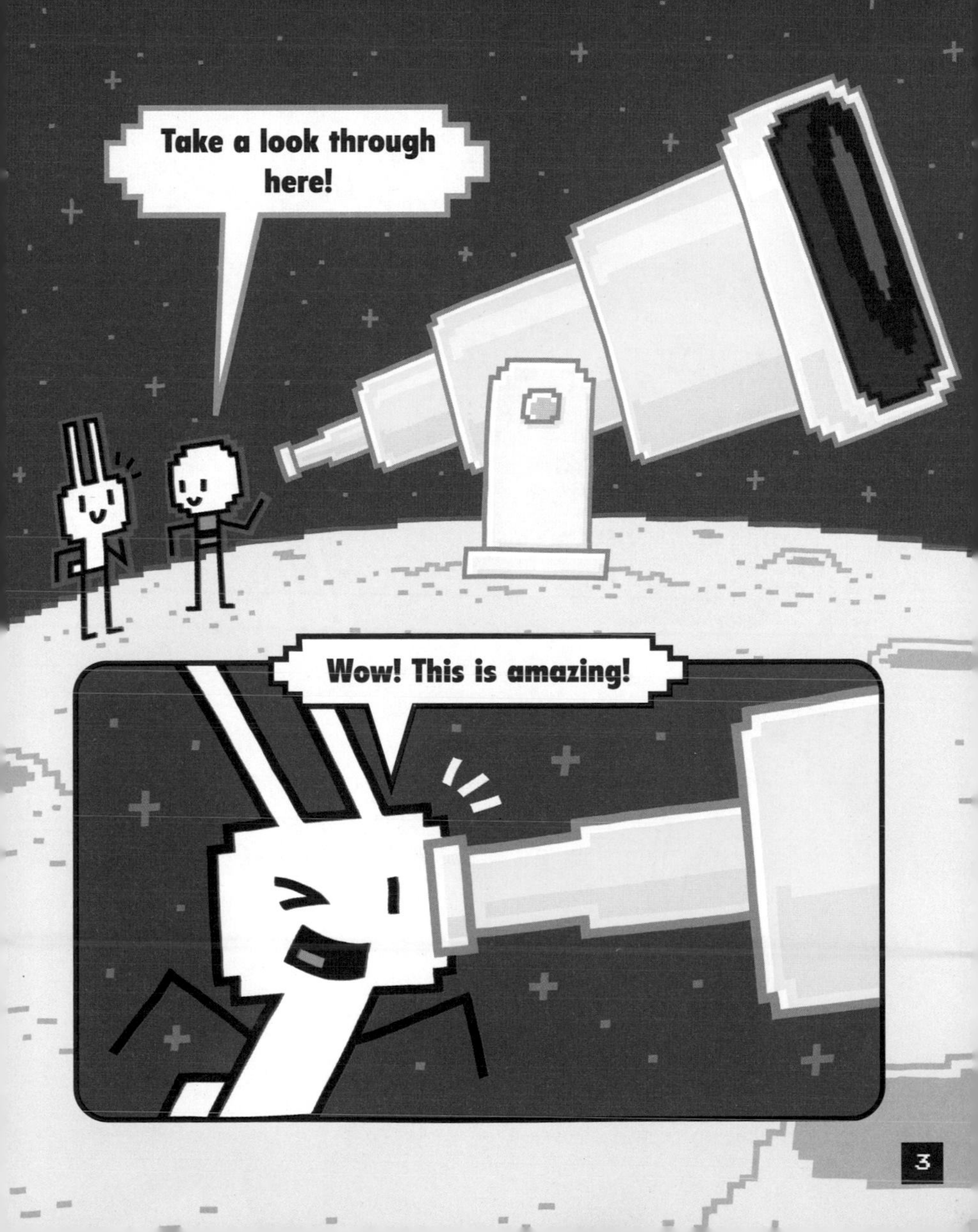

Take a look through here!
Wow! This is amazing!

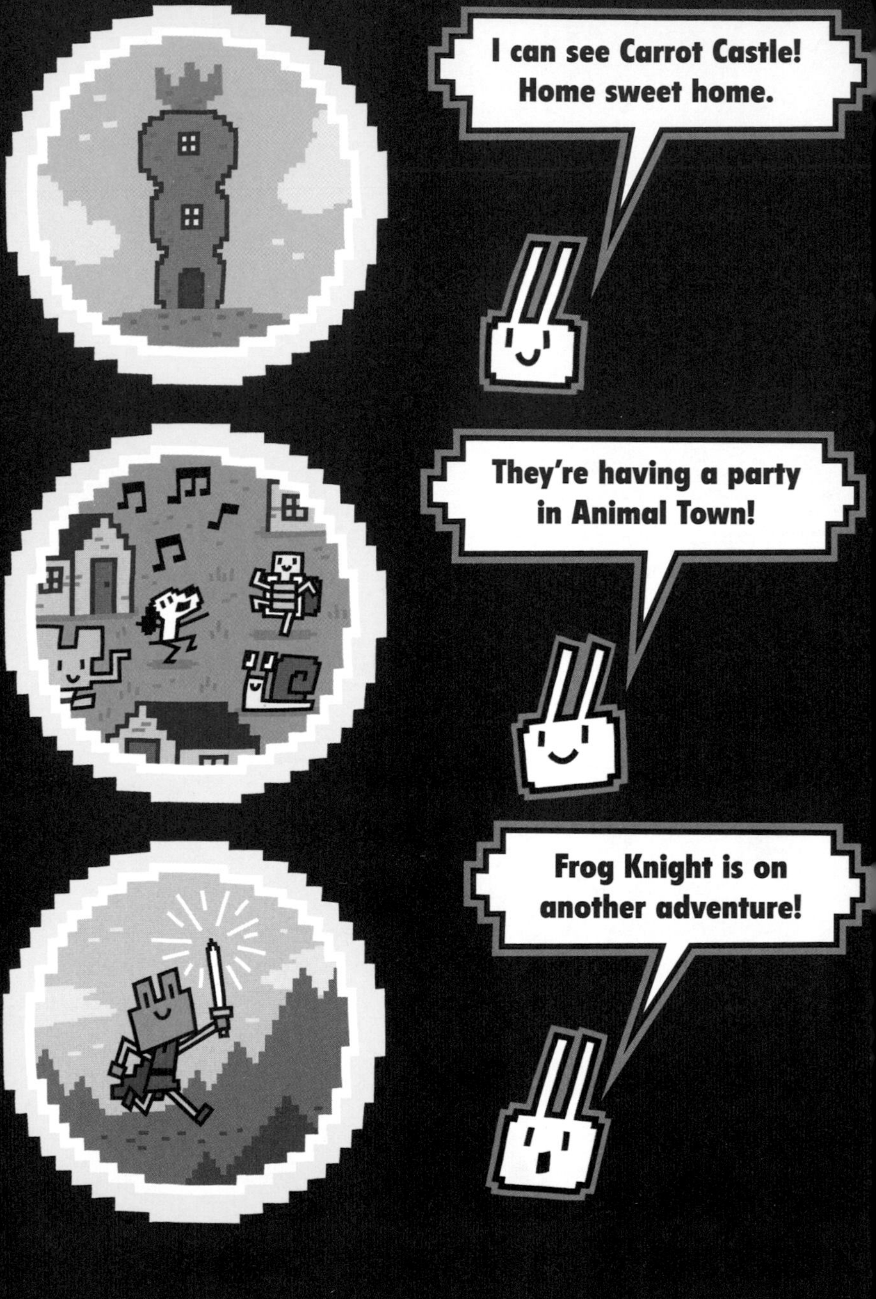
I can see Carrot Castle! Home sweet home.
They're having a party in Animal Town!
Frog Knight is on another adventure!

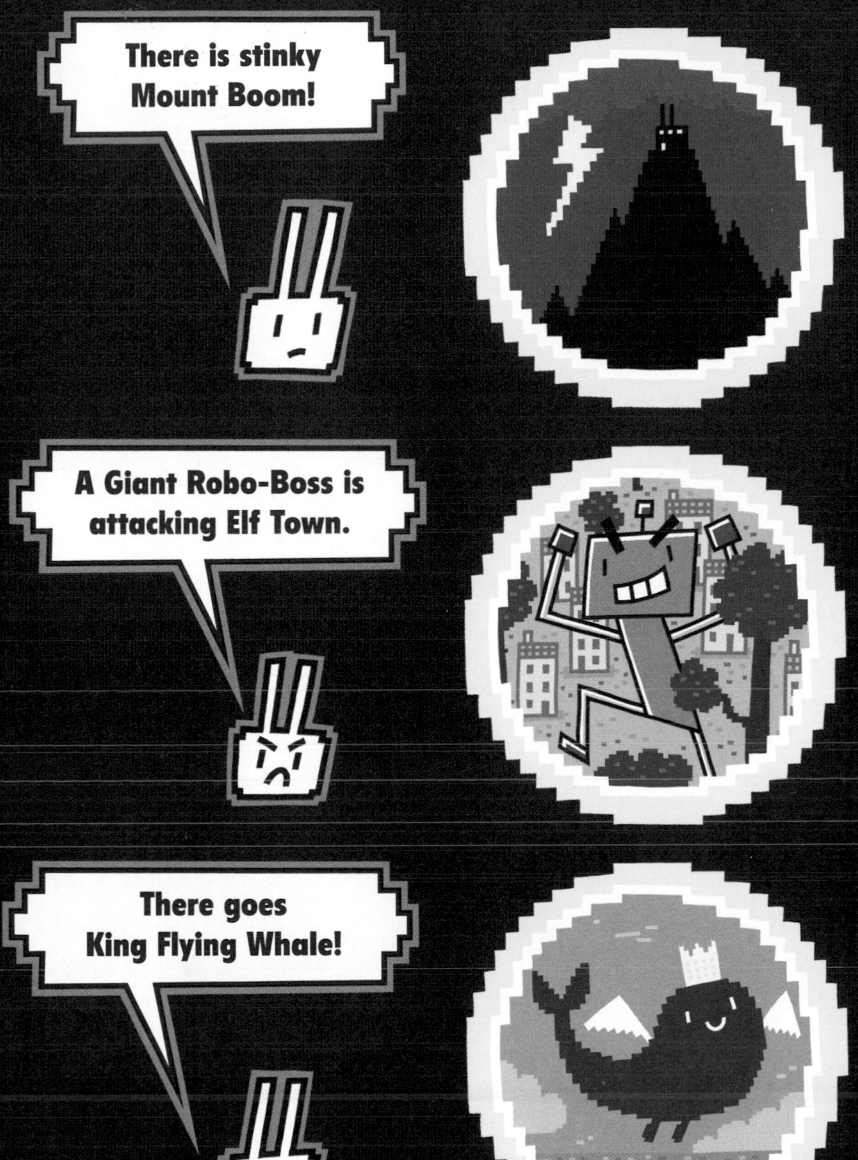
There is stinky Mount Boom!
A Giant Robo-Boss is attacking Elf Town.
There goes King Flying Whale!

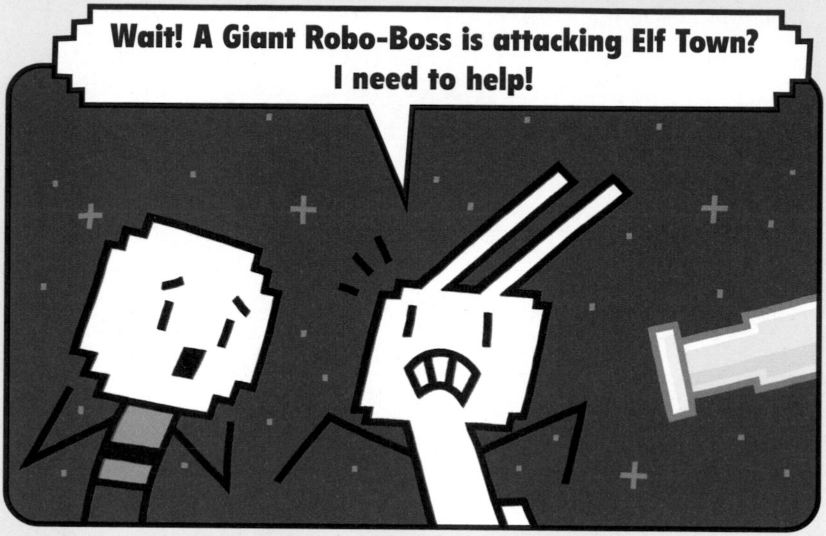
Wait! A Giant Robo-Boss is attacking Elf Town? I need to help!

Super Rabbit Boy races toward Moon Girl's travel cannon.

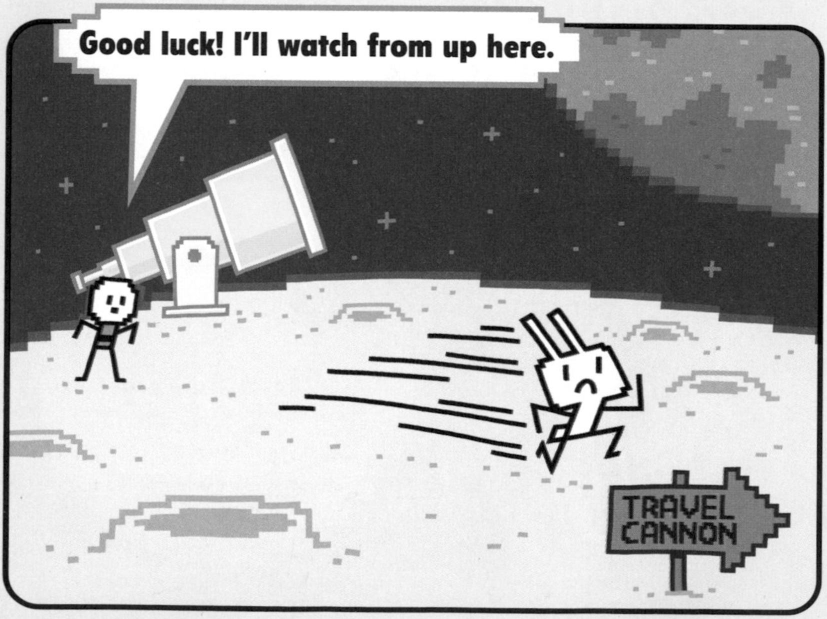
Good luck! I'll watch from up here.
TRAVEL CANNON

Super Rabbit Boy hops into the travel cannon.

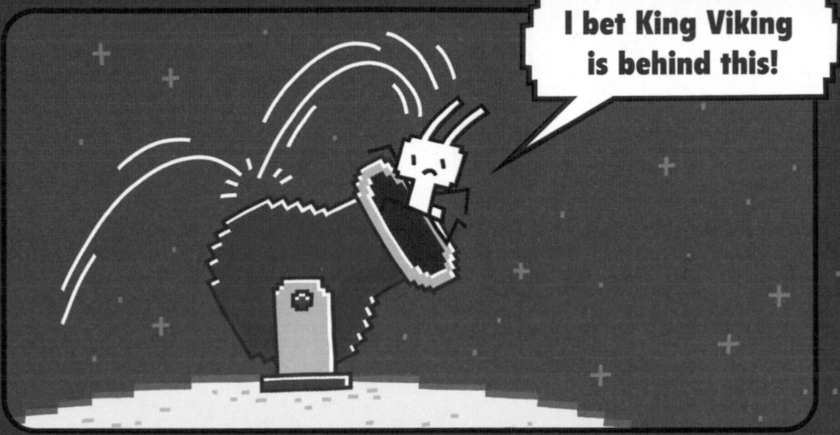
I bet King Viking is behind this!

The travel cannon blasts Super Rabbit Boy toward Super World.

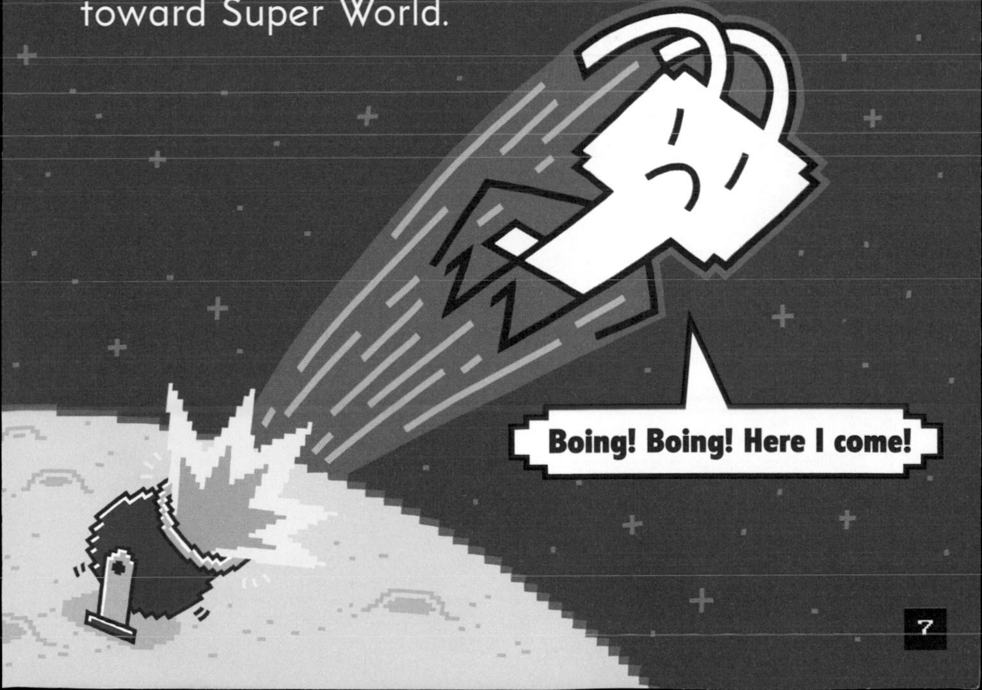
Boing! Boing! Here I come!

2 BIG TROUBLE IN ELF TOWN!

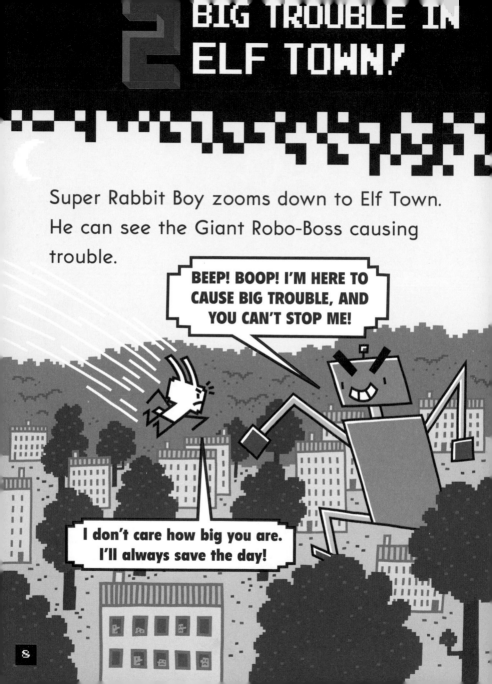

Super Rabbit Boy zooms down to Elf Town. He can see the Giant Robo-Boss causing trouble.

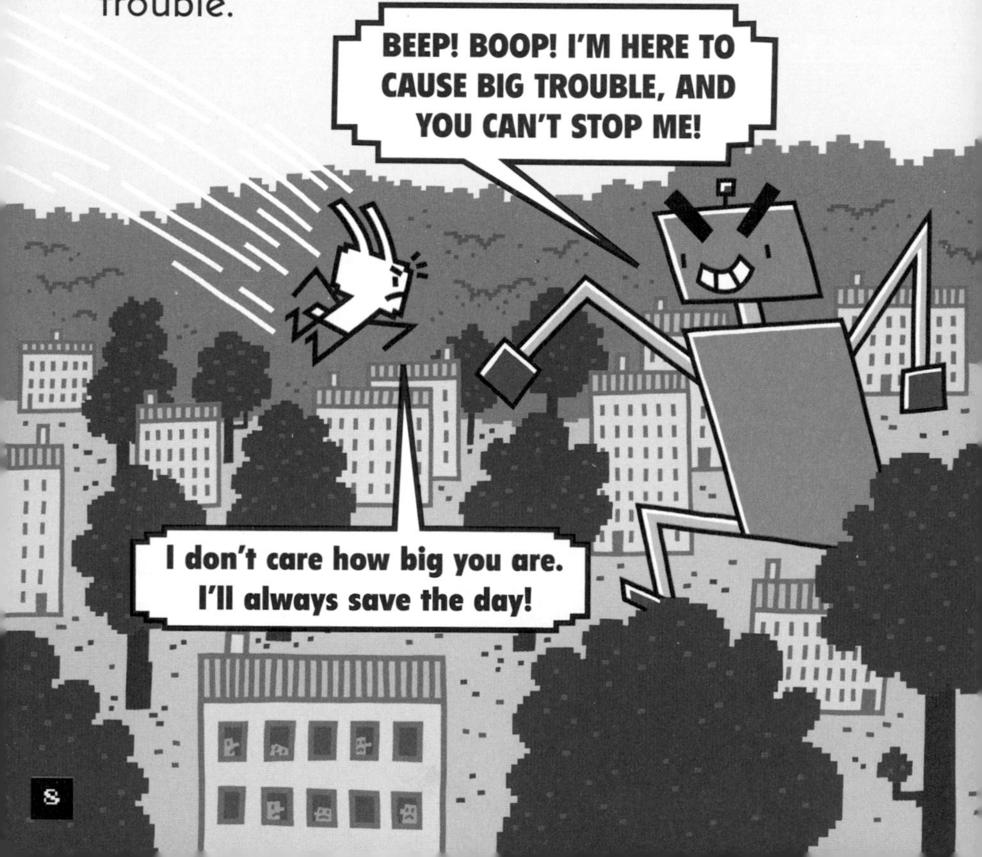
BEEP! BOOP! I'M HERE TO CAUSE BIG TROUBLE, AND YOU CAN'T STOP ME!
I don't care how big you are. I'll always save the day!

He lands right in the center of town. The Giant Robo-Boss looms over him.

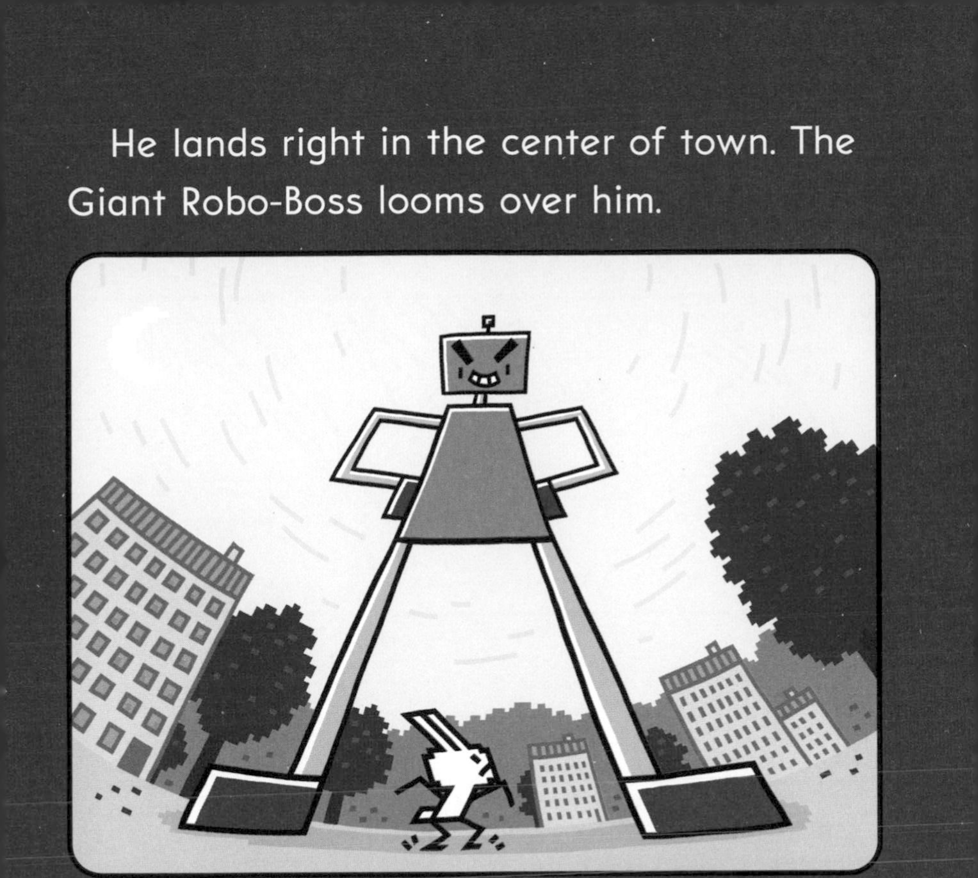

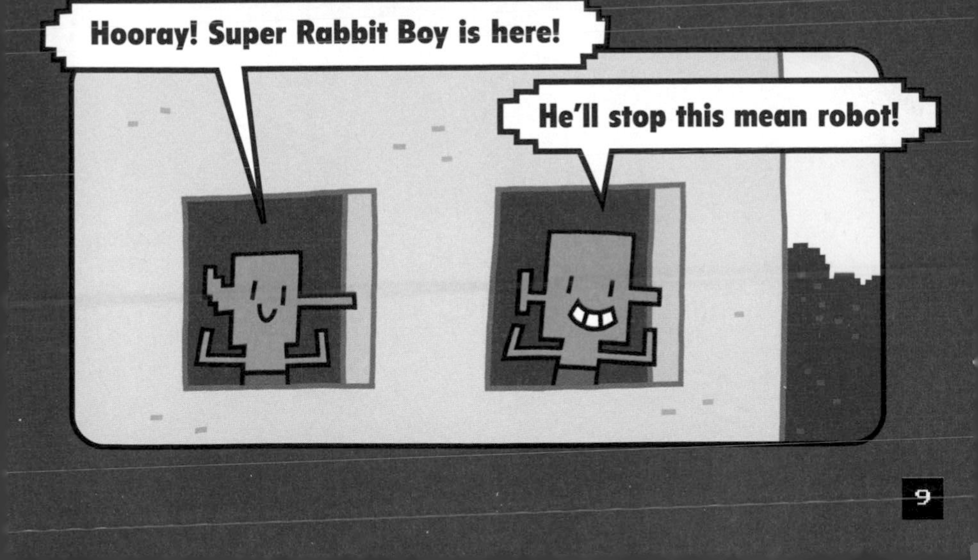
Hooray! Super Rabbit Boy is here!
He'll stop this mean robot!

The Giant Robo-Boss tries to stomp on Super Rabbit Boy. But Super Rabbit Boy hops out of the way.

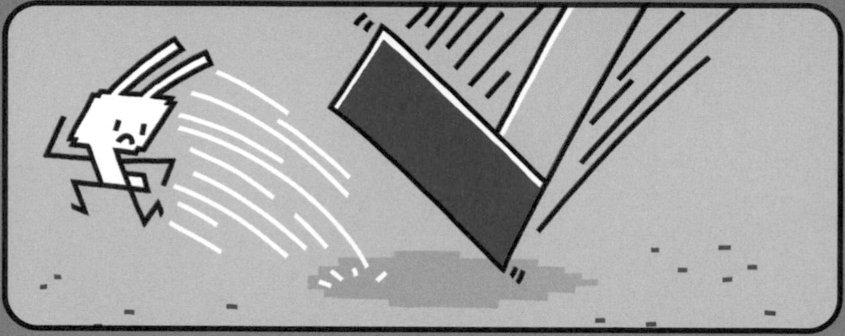

It keeps trying, but Super Rabbit Boy is too quick.

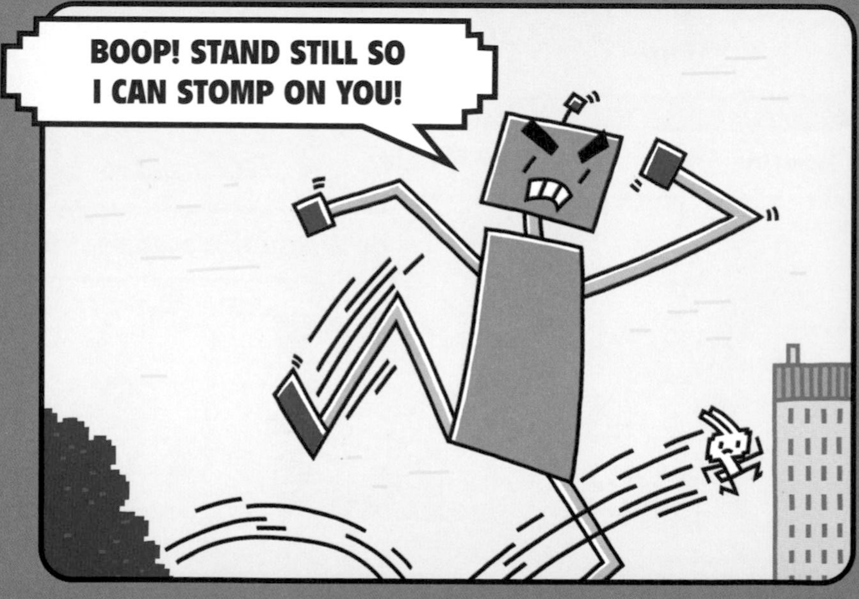
BOOP! STAND STILL SO I CAN STOMP ON YOU!

Super Rabbit Boy starts to hop around in circles. He makes the Giant Robo-Boss spin around and around.

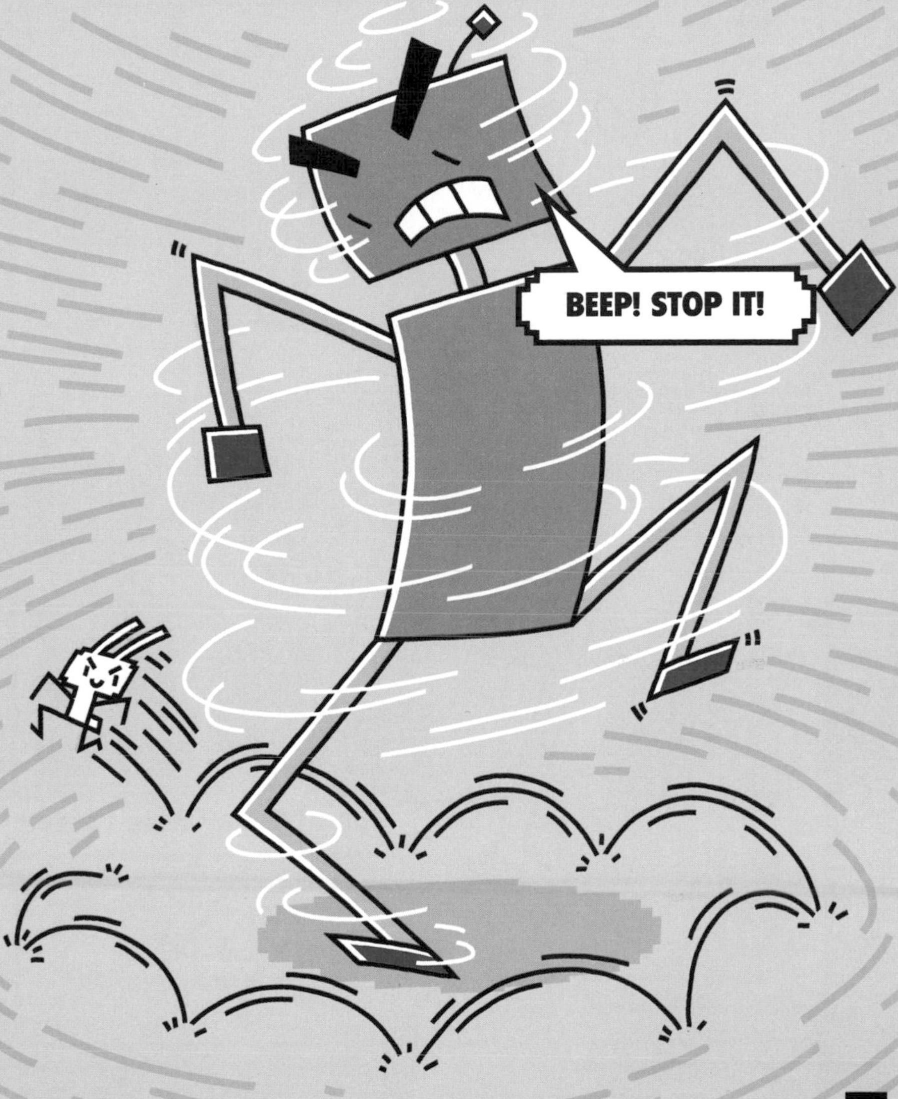
BEEP! STOP IT!

All that spinning has made the Giant Robo-Boss dizzy. It starts to wobble.

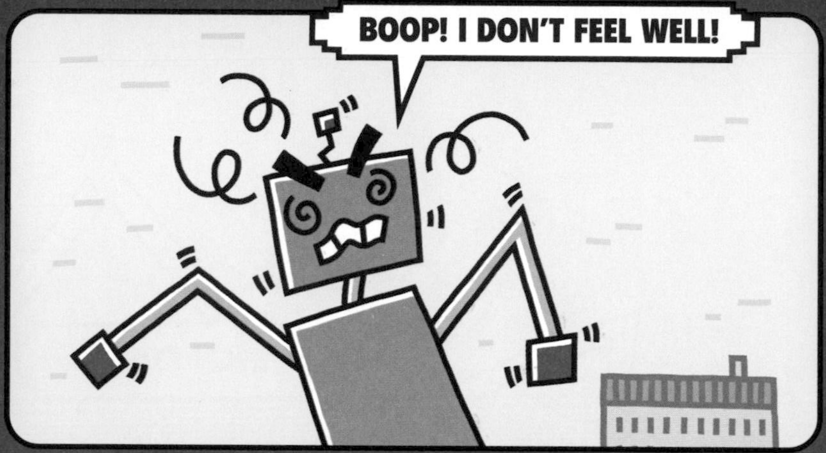
BOOP! I DON'T FEEL WELL!

Super Rabbit Boy quickly climbs the wobbling robot.

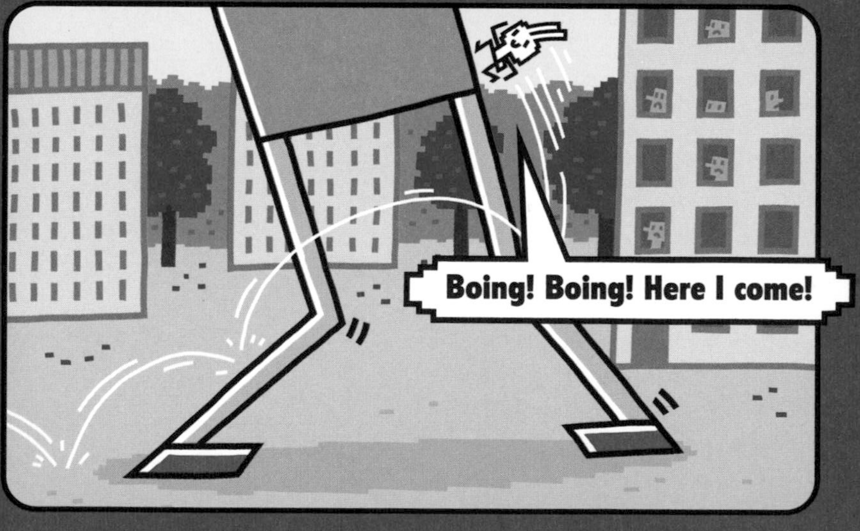
Boing! Boing! Here I come!

He climbs all the way up to the Giant Robo-Boss's head. He uses his Super Jump to push the Giant Robo-Boss over.

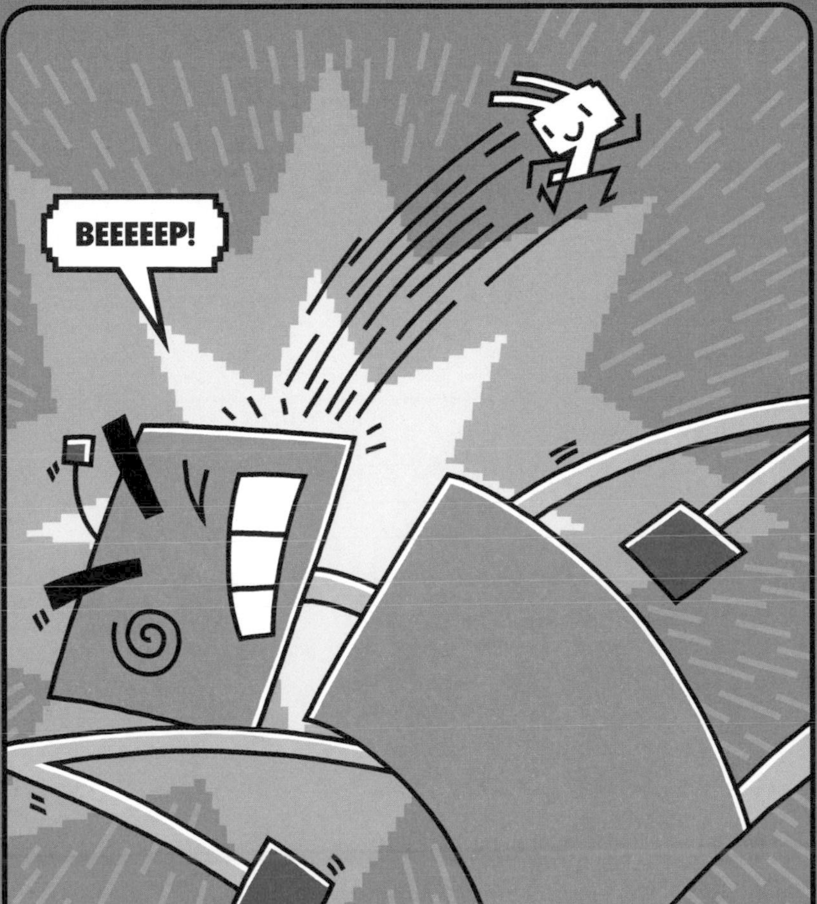
BEEEEEP!

The Giant Robo-Boss crashes to the ground. Super Rabbit Boy has won!

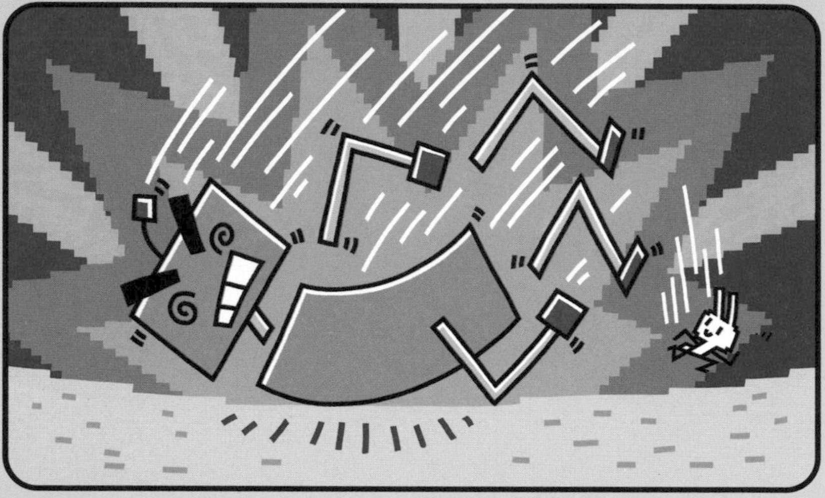

But he has no time to celebrate. A voice in the sky calls out to him.

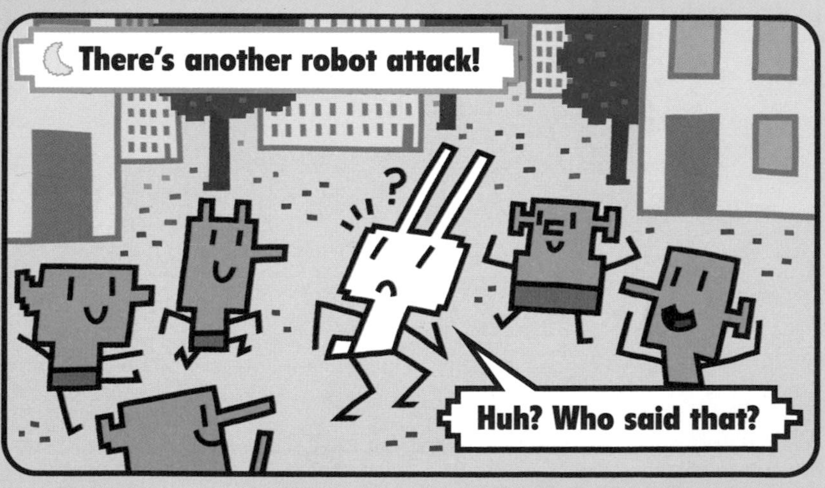
There's another robot attack!
Huh? Who said that?

3 ROBOTS IN THE WOODS

Moon Girl is using her telescope's built-in megaphone to talk to Super Rabbit Boy.

It's me, Moon Girl. Up here!

I just spotted more trouble through my telescope!

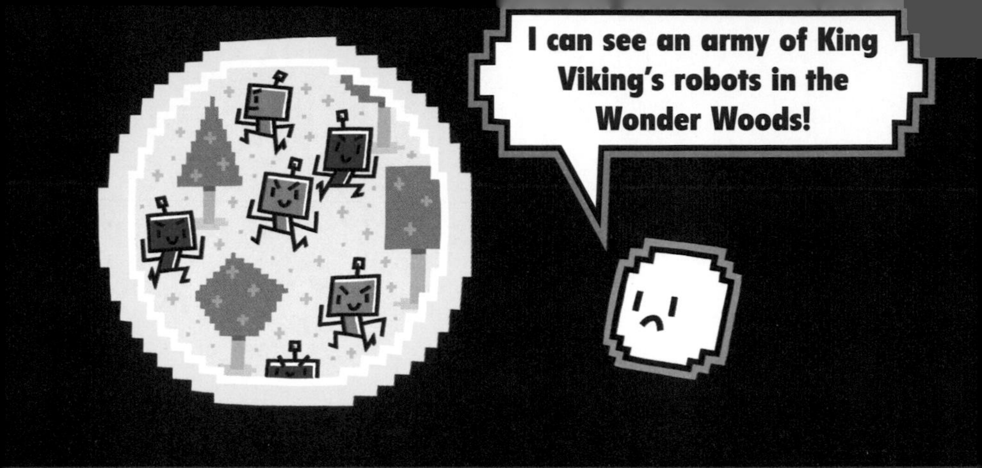
I can see an army of King Viking's robots in the Wonder Woods!

Super Rabbit Boy dashes toward one of Super World's many travel cannons. They are a fast way to travel long distances.

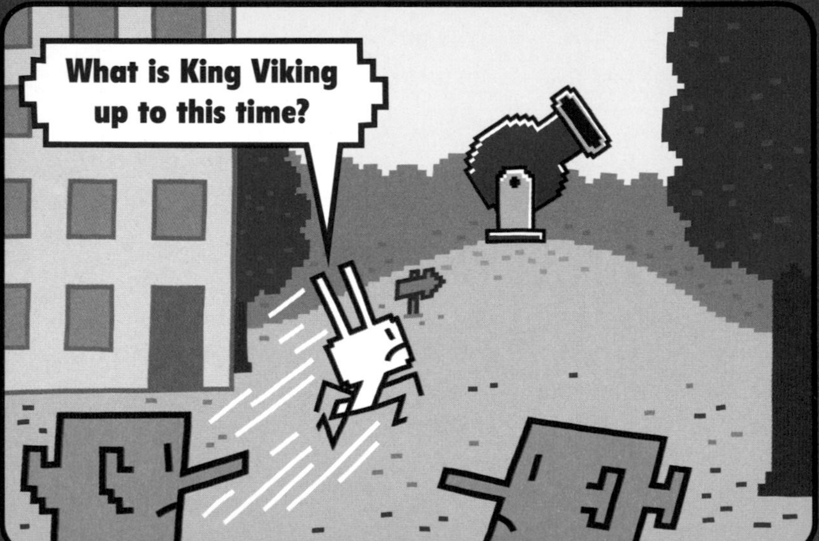
What is King Viking up to this time?

He hops into the travel cannon and blasts off toward the Wonder Woods.

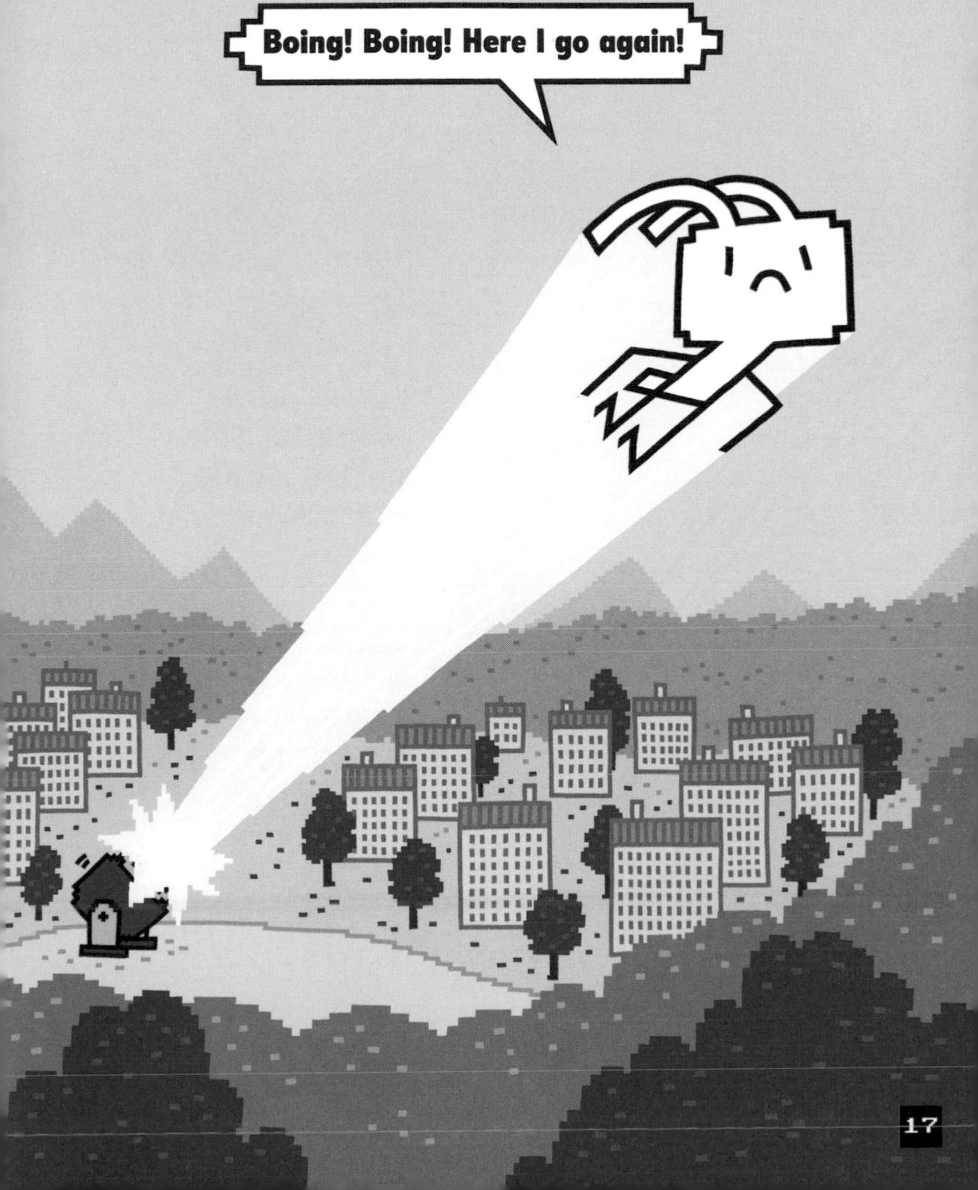
Boing! Boing! Here I go again!

Super Rabbit Boy lands in the Wonder Woods. There is no sign of King Viking, but his robots are everywhere!

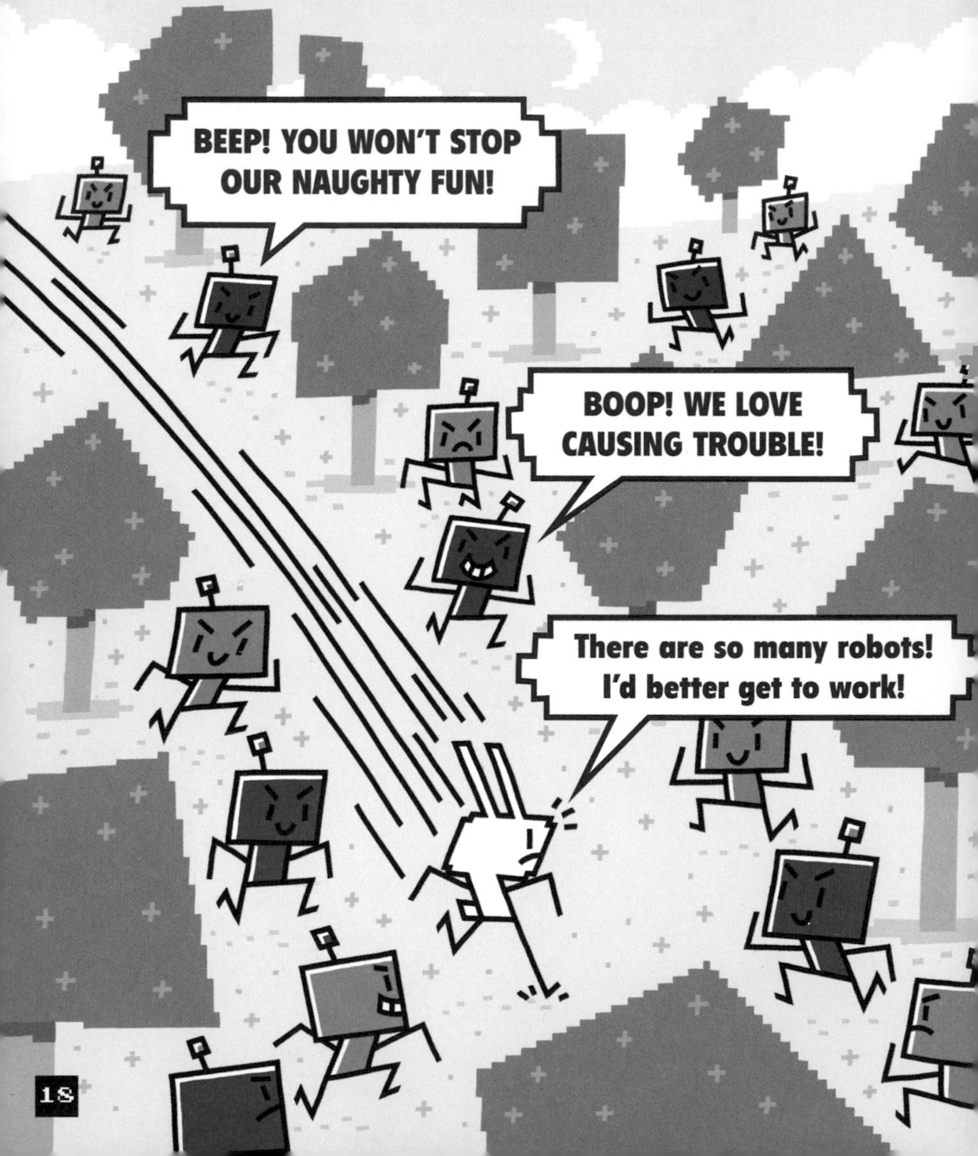
BEEP! YOU WON'T STOP OUR NAUGHTY FUN!
BOOP! WE LOVE CAUSING TROUBLE!
There are so many robots! I'd better get to work!

Super Rabbit Boy bounces into action. He uses his Super Jump to stop the robots.

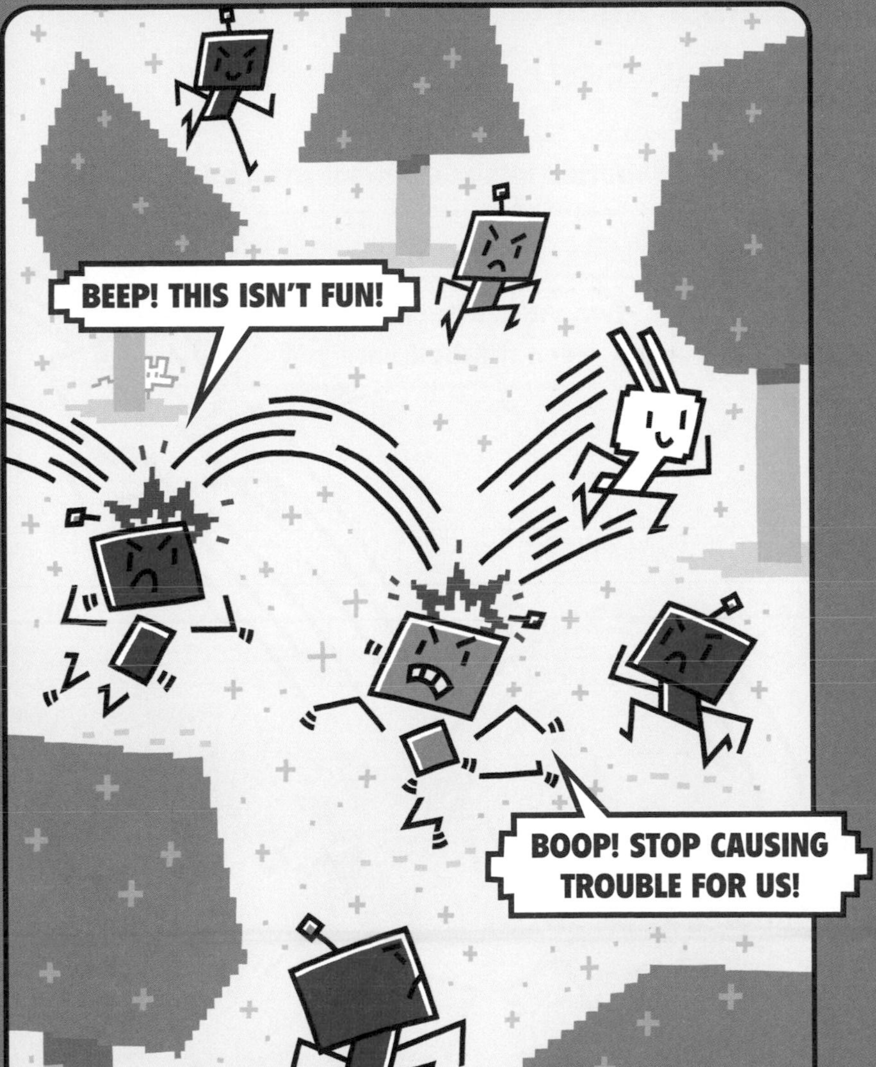
BEEP! THIS ISN'T FUN!
BOOP! STOP CAUSING TROUBLE FOR US!

Super Rabbit Boy is still busy bouncing from robot to robot when Moon Girl calls out again.

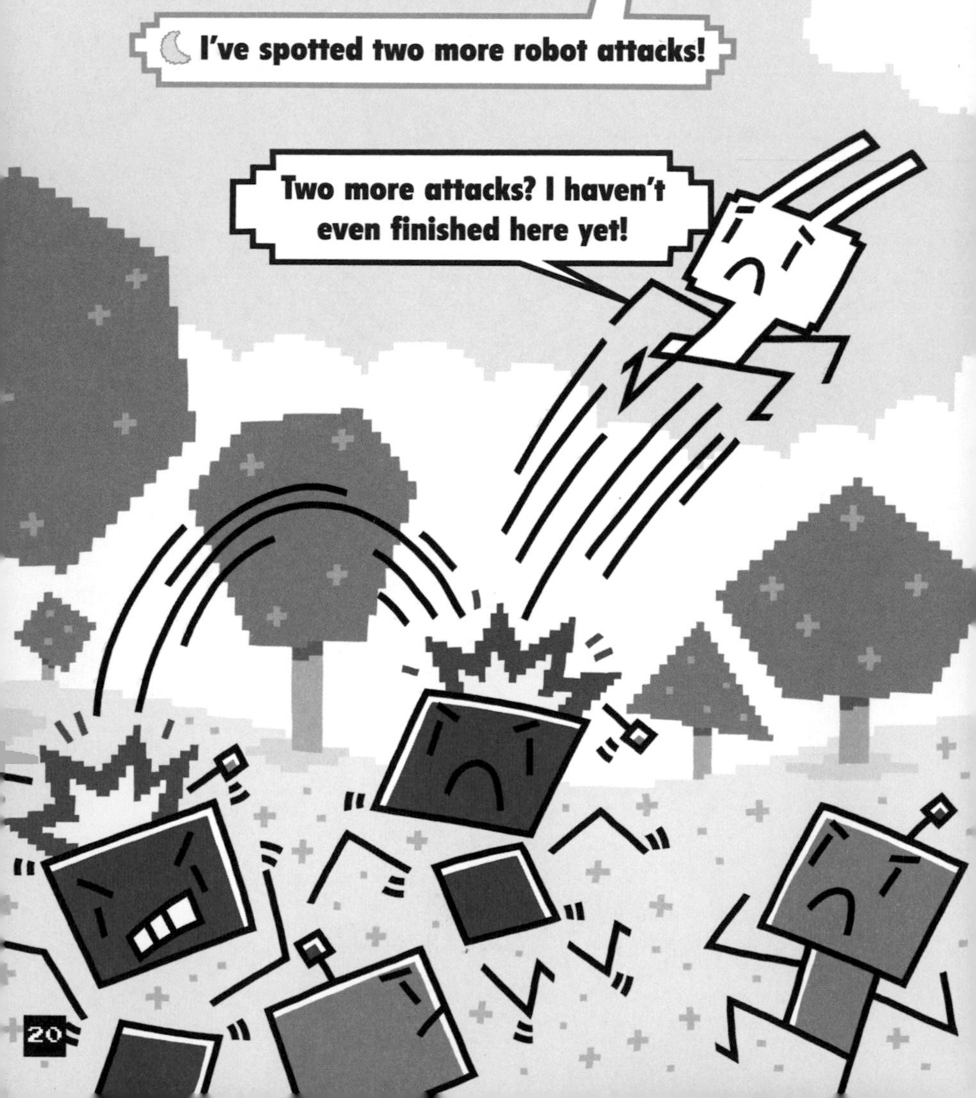
I've spotted two more robot attacks!
Two more attacks? I haven't even finished here yet!

4 A ROCKY SITUATION

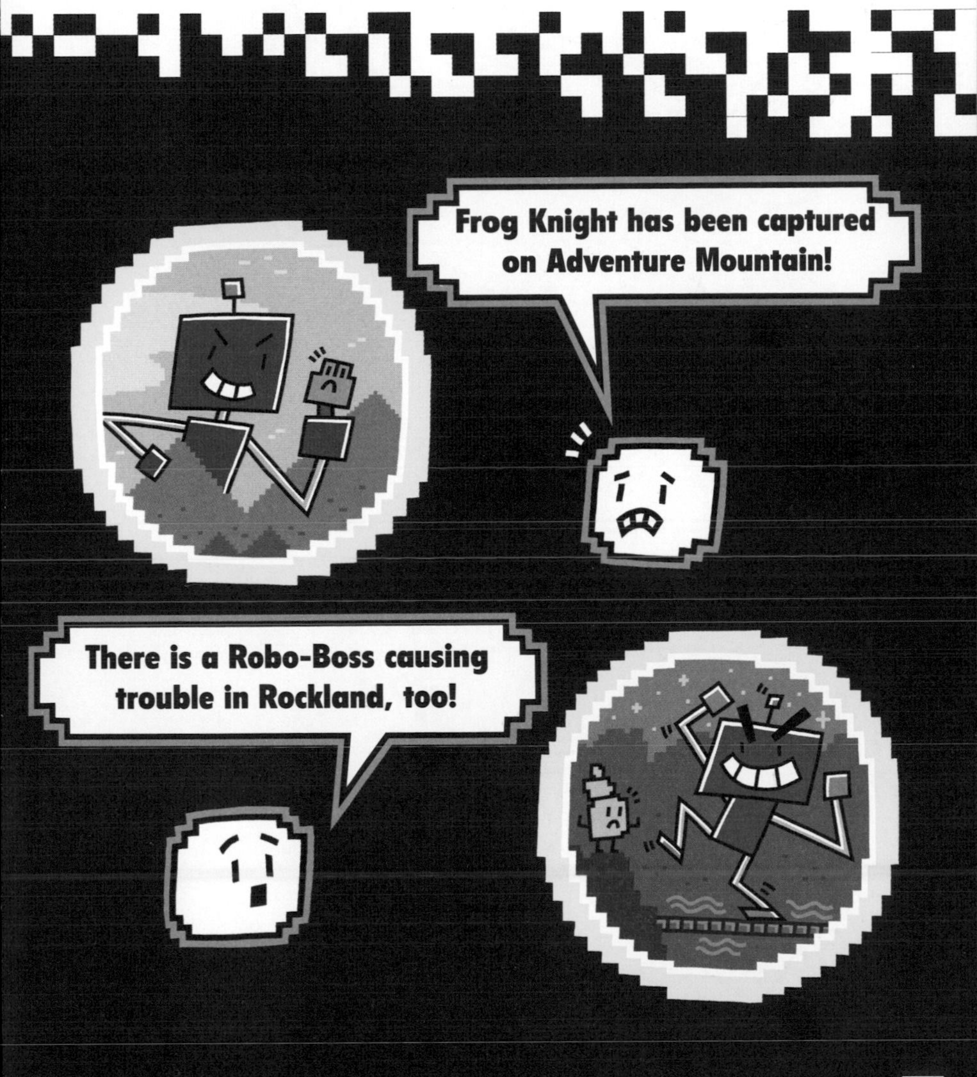

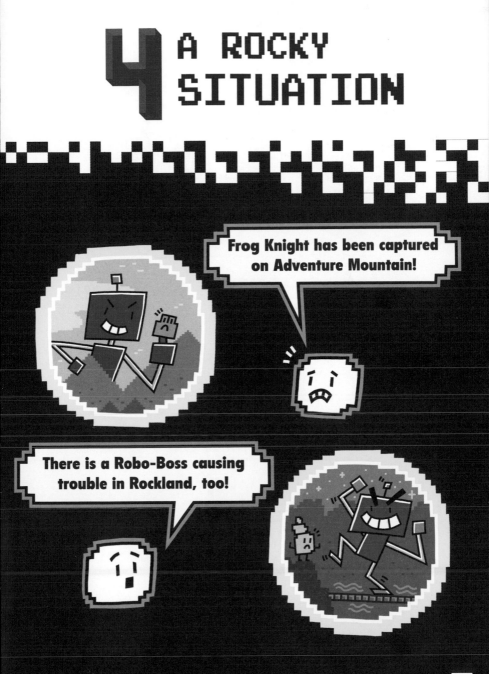

Frog Knight has been captured on Adventure Mountain!
There is a Robo-Boss causing trouble in Rockland, too!

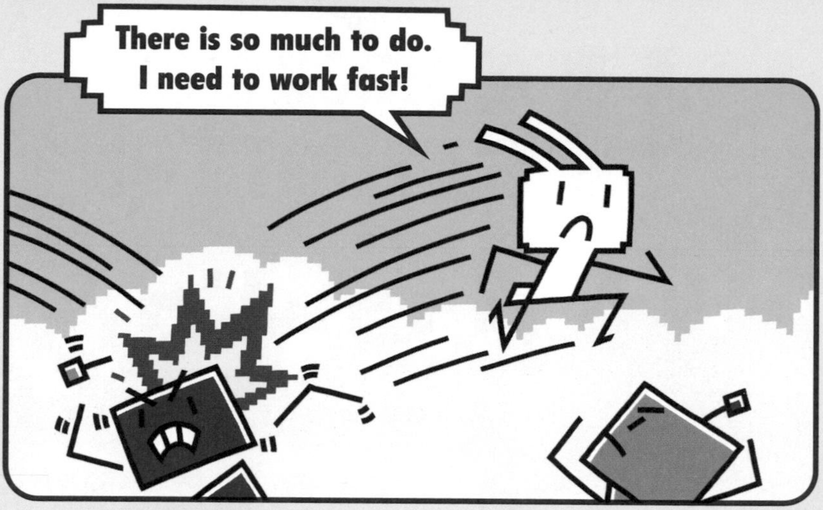
There is so much to do.
I need to work fast!

Super Rabbit Boy defeats the last robot in the Wonder Woods. Then he races off to the nearest travel cannon.

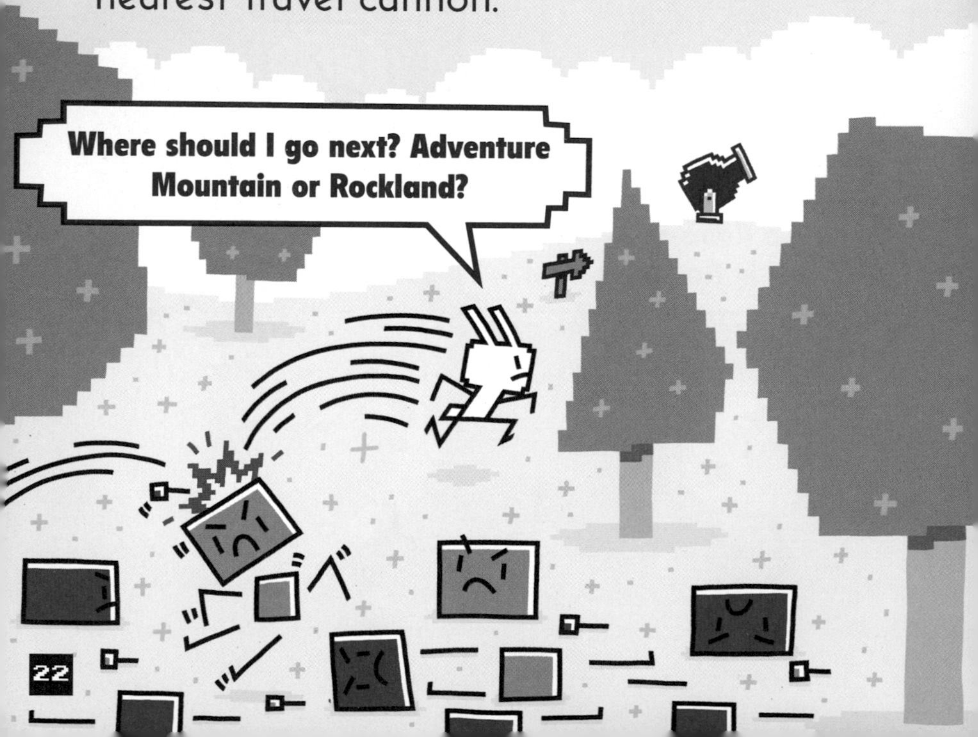
Where should I go next? Adventure Mountain or Rockland?

Super Rabbit Boy decides to go to Rockland first. He blasts off again.

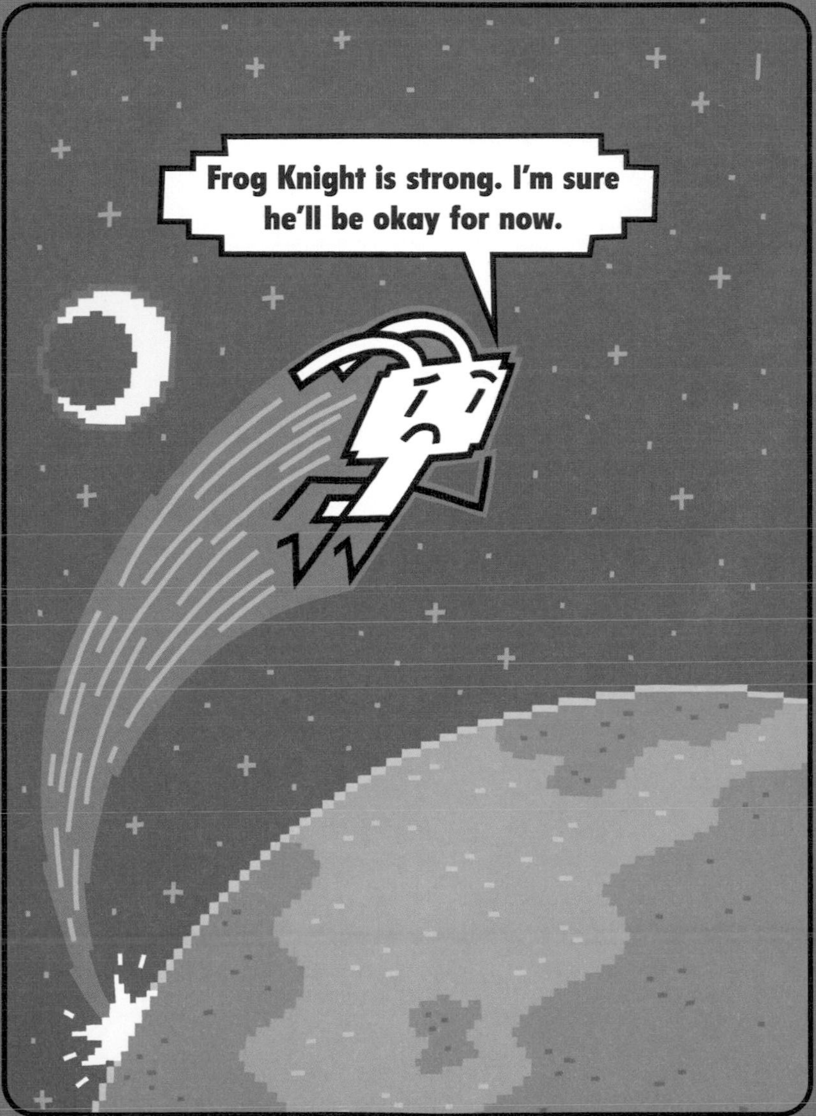
Frog Knight is strong. I'm sure he'll be okay for now.

Super Rabbit Boy arrives in Rockland.

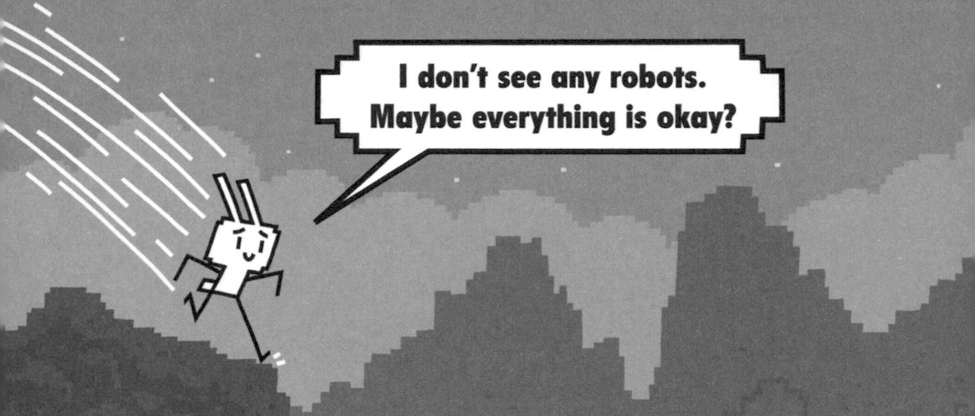
I don't see any robots.
Maybe everything is okay?

A group of rockles runs over to him. They are very worried.

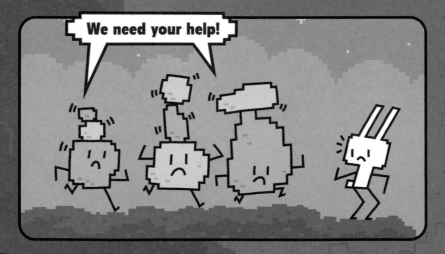

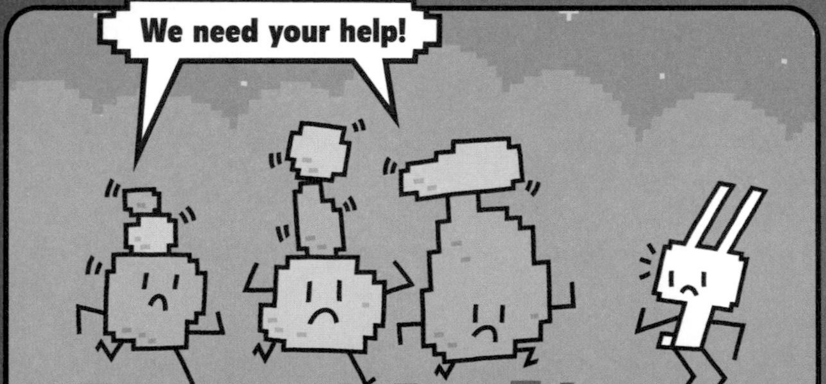
We need your help!

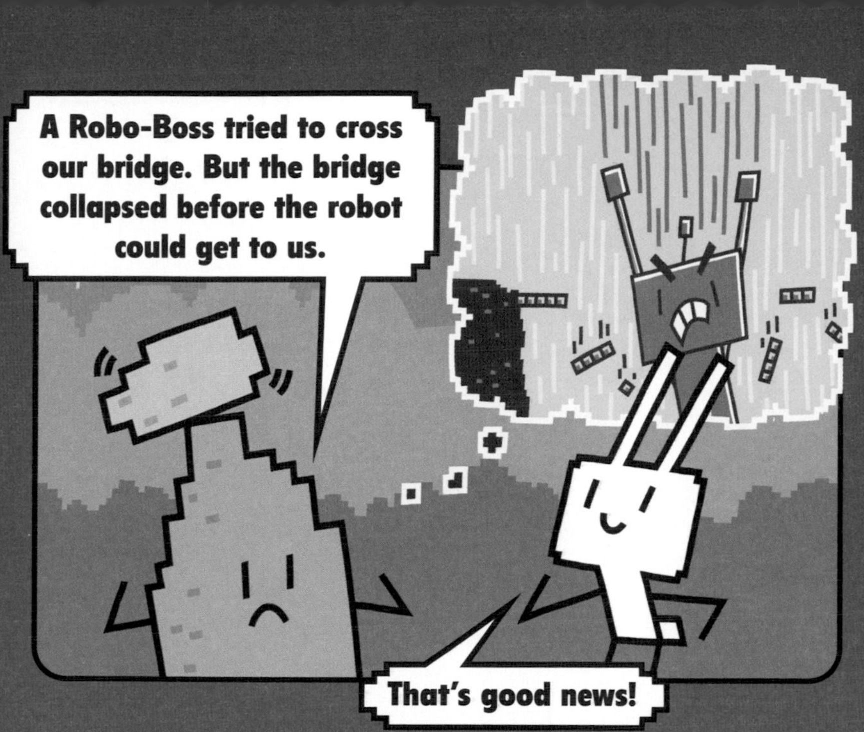
A Robo-Boss tried to cross our bridge. But the bridge collapsed before the robot could get to us.
That's good news!

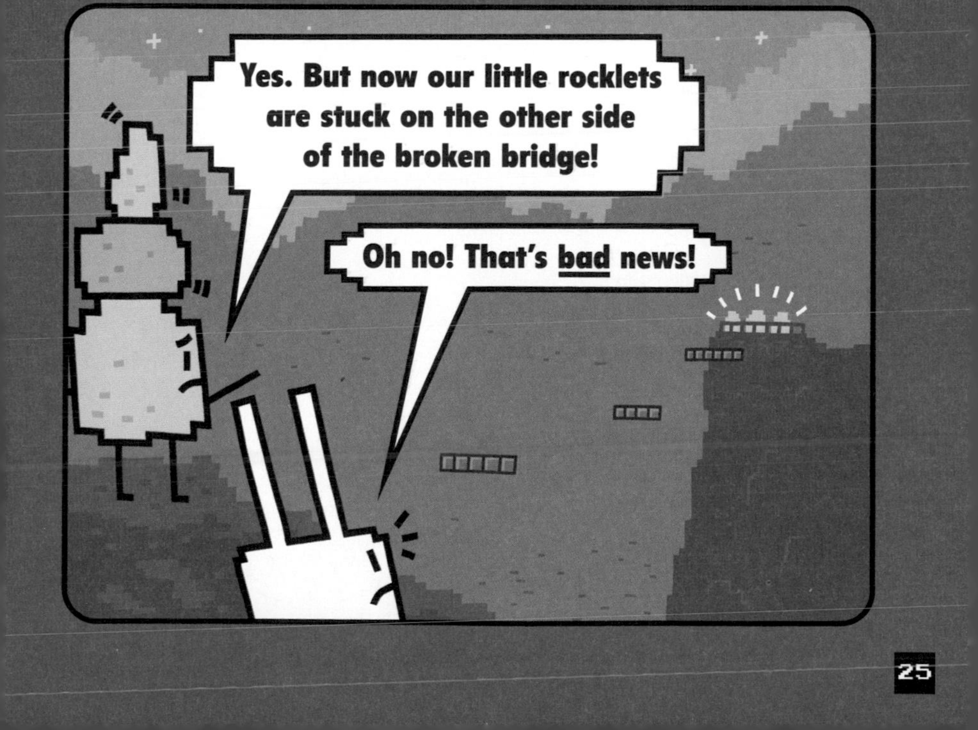
Yes. But now our little rocklets are stuck on the other side of the broken bridge!
Oh no! That's bad news!

5 ROCK-A-BYE BABIES

Super Rabbit Boy looks at the broken bridge. There is a deep pit underneath it.

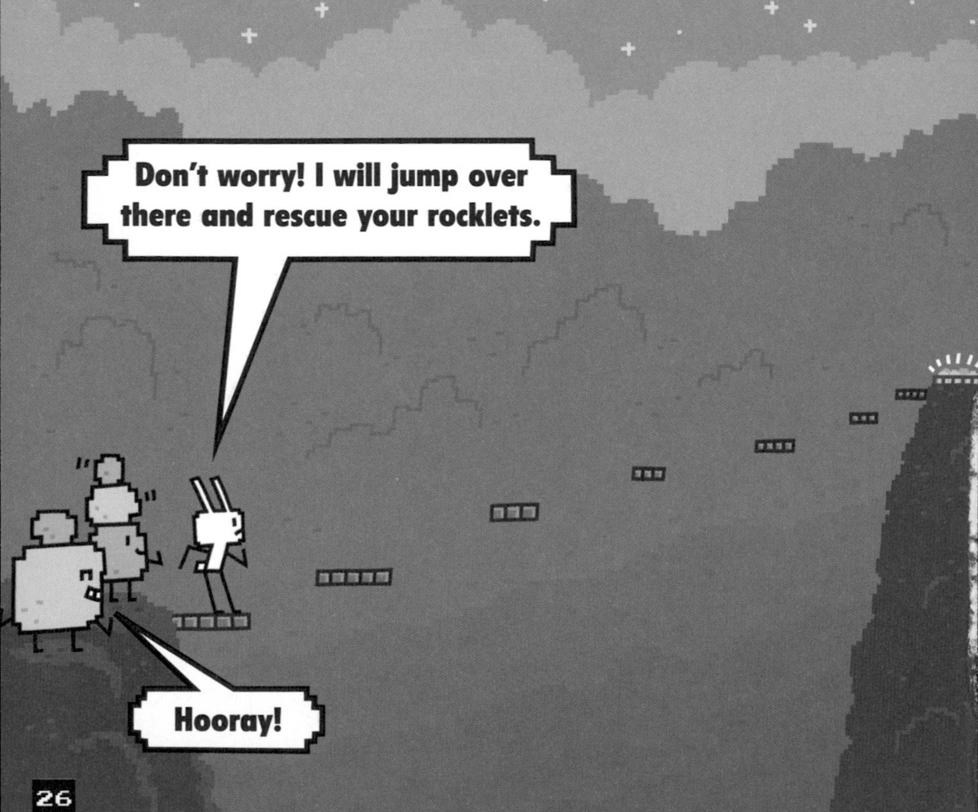

Don't worry! I will jump over there and rescue your rocklets.
Hooray!

Super Rabbit Boy hops over the broken bridge toward the rocklets.

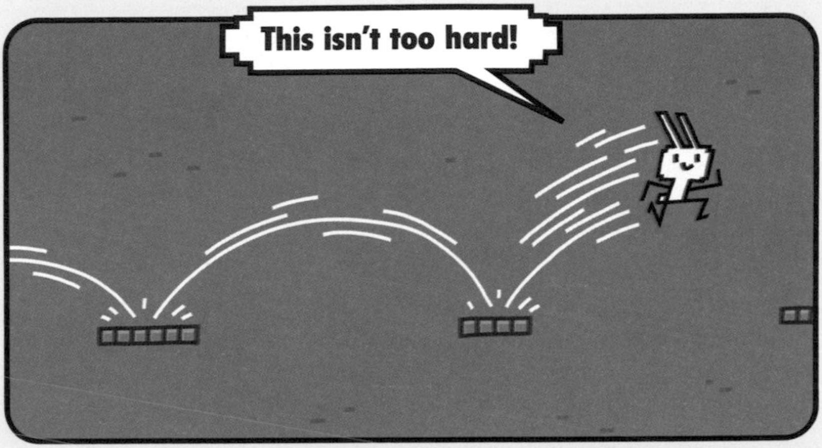
This isn't too hard!

He lands on the other side. The little rocklets are happy to see him.

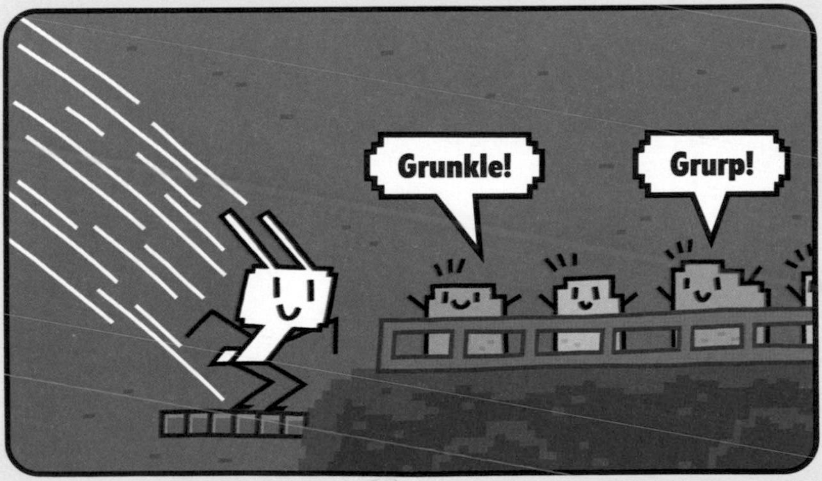
Grunkle!
Grurp!

Super Rabbit Boy picks up the first rocklet. It's super heavy!

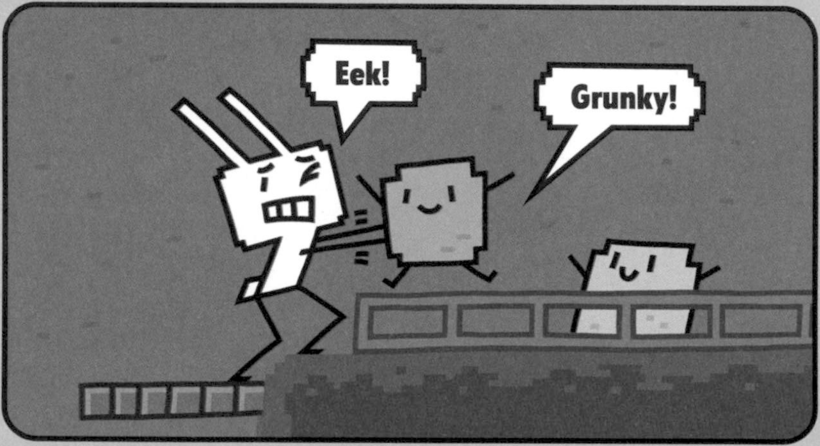
Eek!
Grunky!

He starts to hop back.

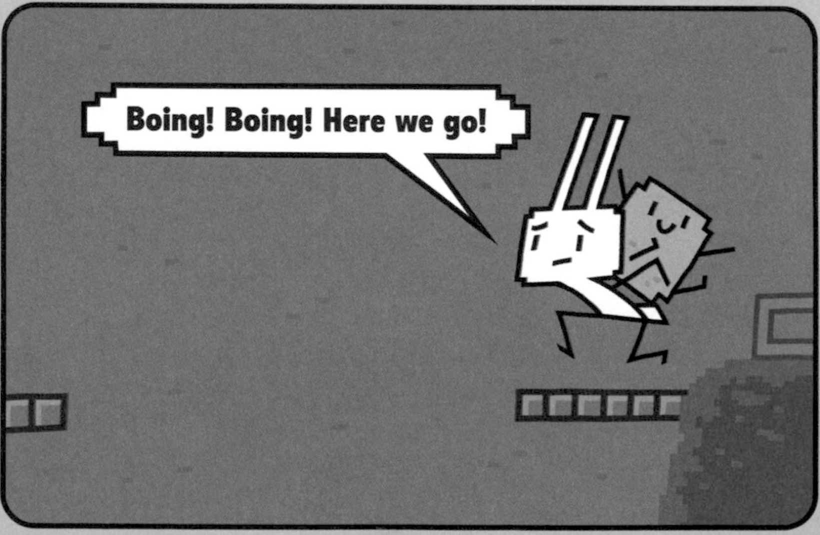
Boing! Boing! Here we go!

It's much harder to jump across while carrying the rocklet.

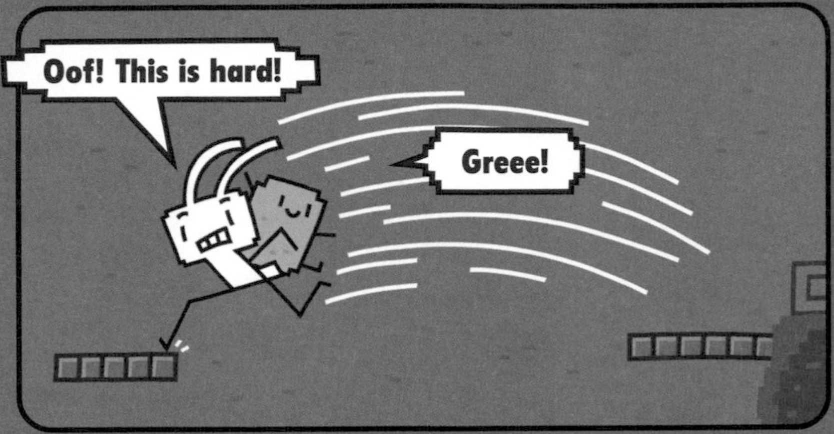
Oof! This is hard!
Greee!

They are almost across, but there is one last big jump.

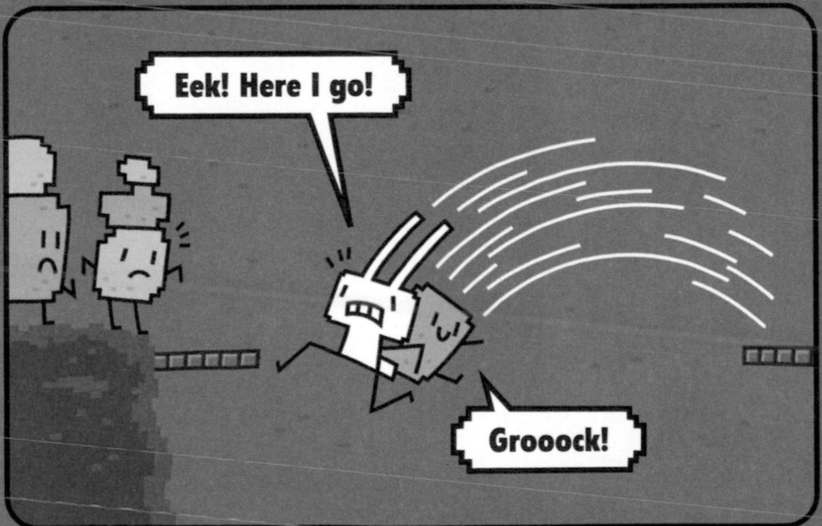
Eek! Here I go!
Grooock!

The rockles grab them just in time.

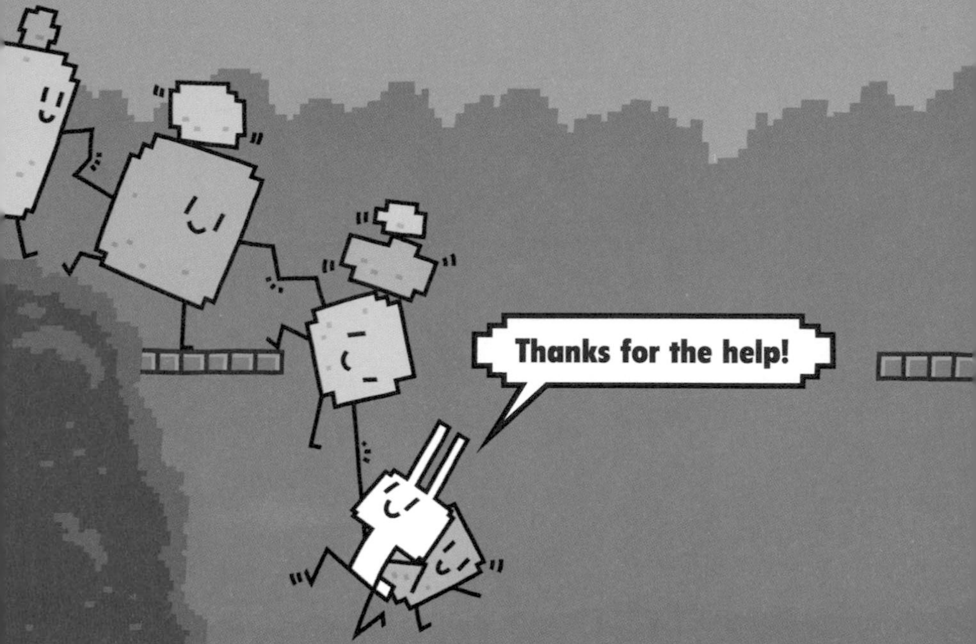
Thanks for the help!

Super Rabbit Boy hops back over the broken bridge.

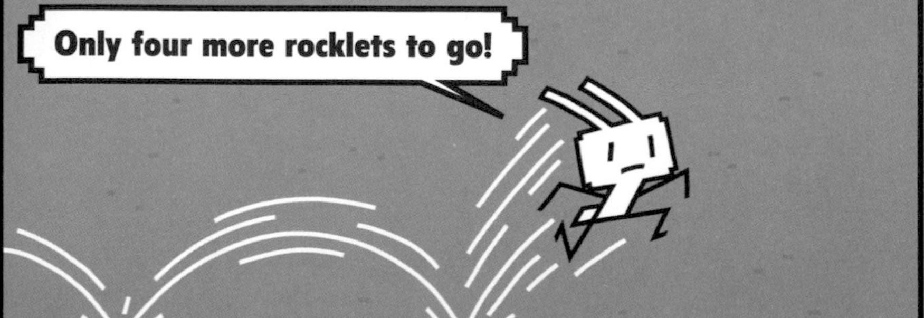
Only four more rocklets to go!

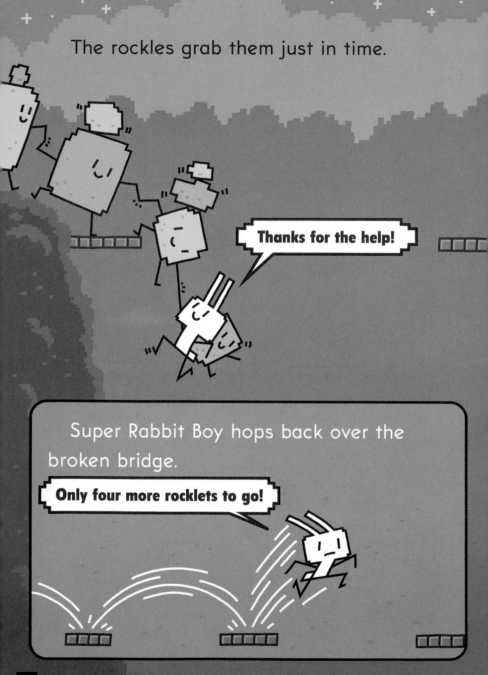

He jumps back and forth across the deep pit. One by one, he saves them.

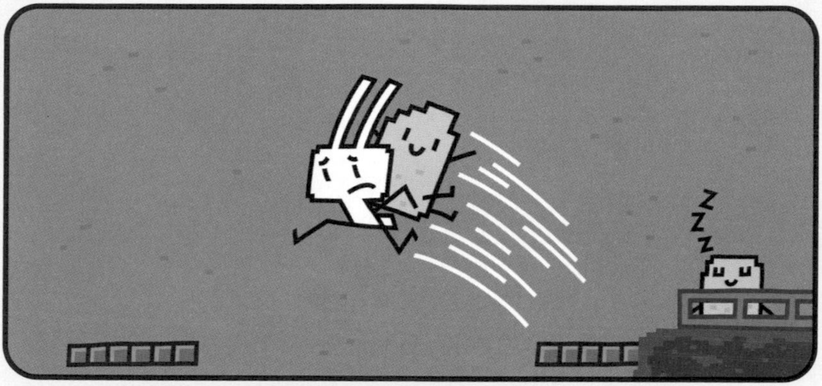
Z
Z
Z

He is almost back with the last baby when Moon Girl's voice calls out to him again.

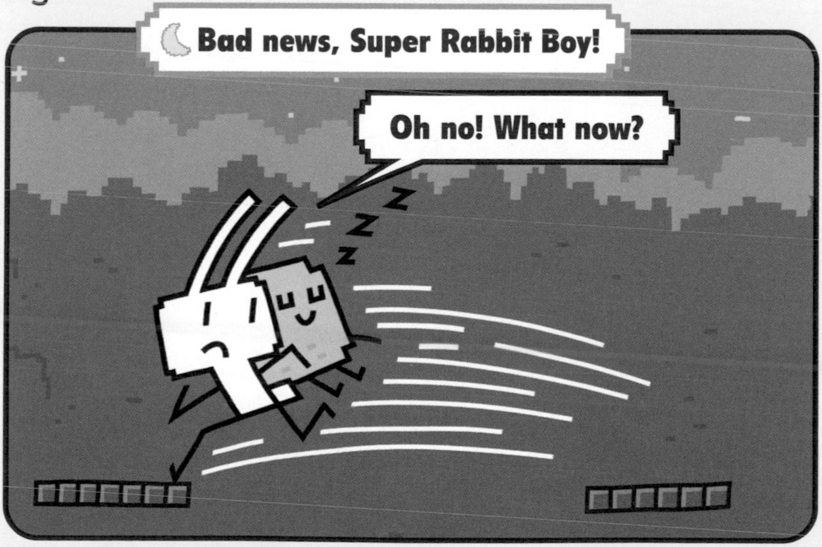
Bad news, Super Rabbit Boy!
Oh no! What now?
Z
Z
Z

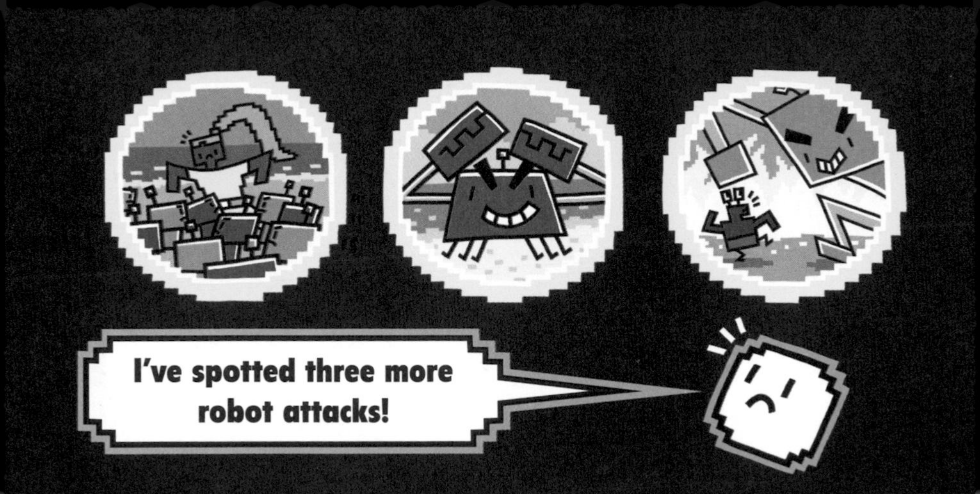
I've spotted three more
robot attacks!

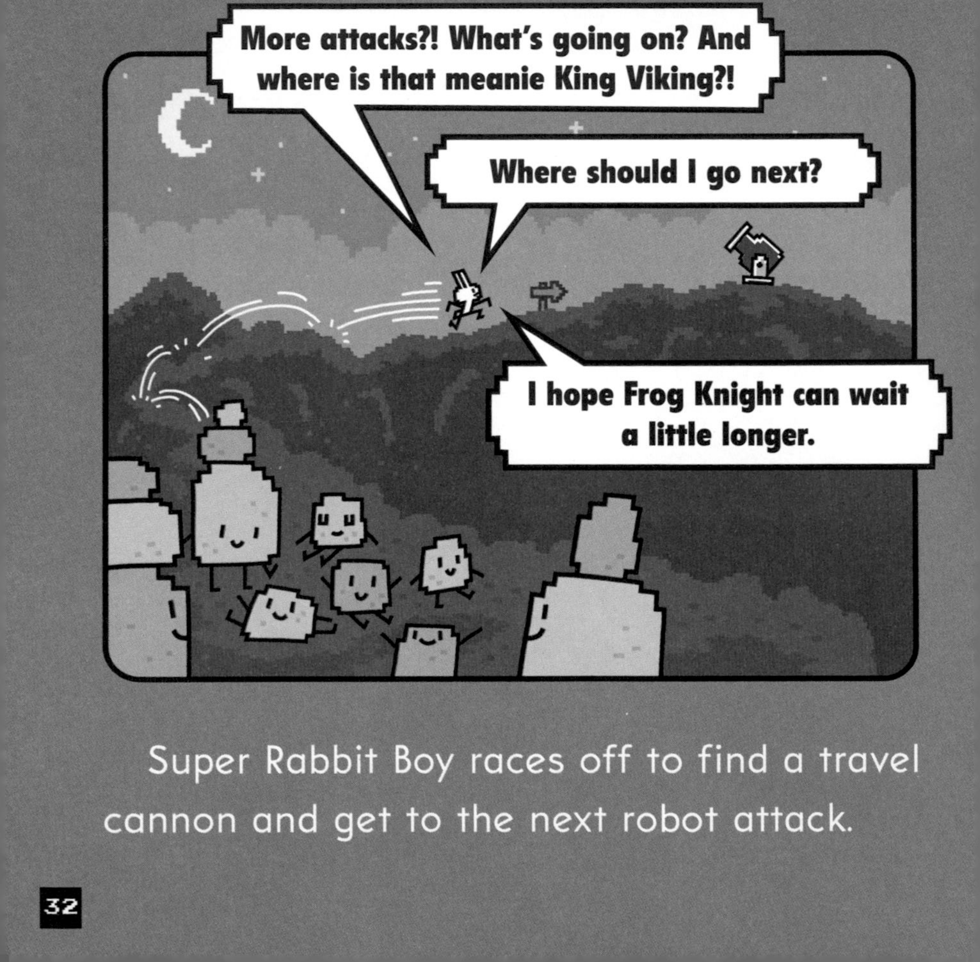
More attacks?! What's going on? And
where is that meanie King Viking?!
Where should I go next?
I hope Frog Knight can wait
a little longer.

Super Rabbit Boy races off to find a travel cannon and get to the next robot attack.

6 THE MULTI-PLAN PLAN

Super Rabbit Boy blasts off toward another robot attack.

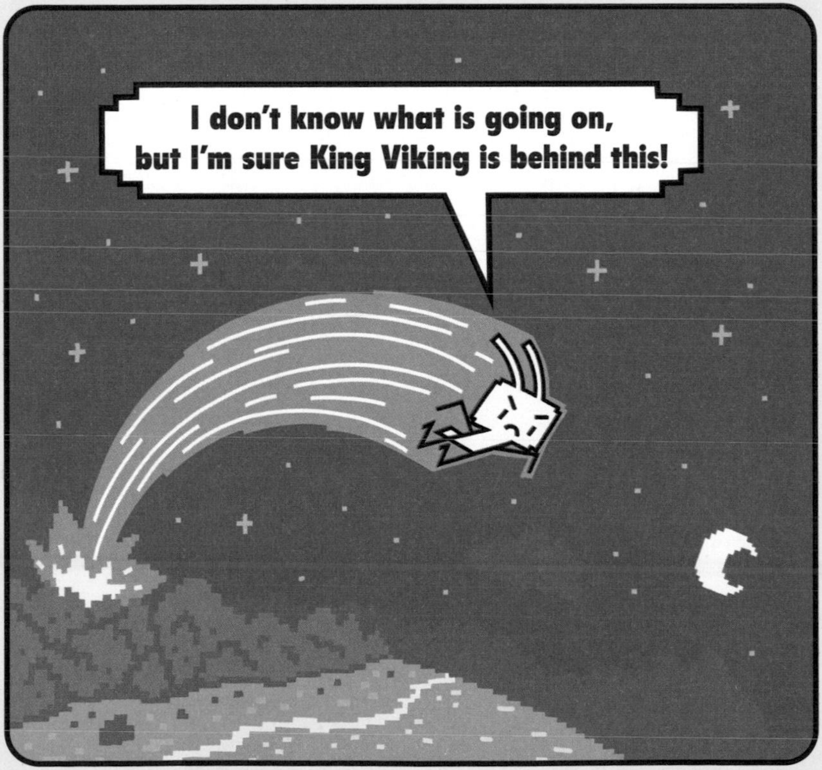
I don't know what is going on, but I'm sure King Viking is behind this!

Super Rabbit Boy travels across all of Super World.

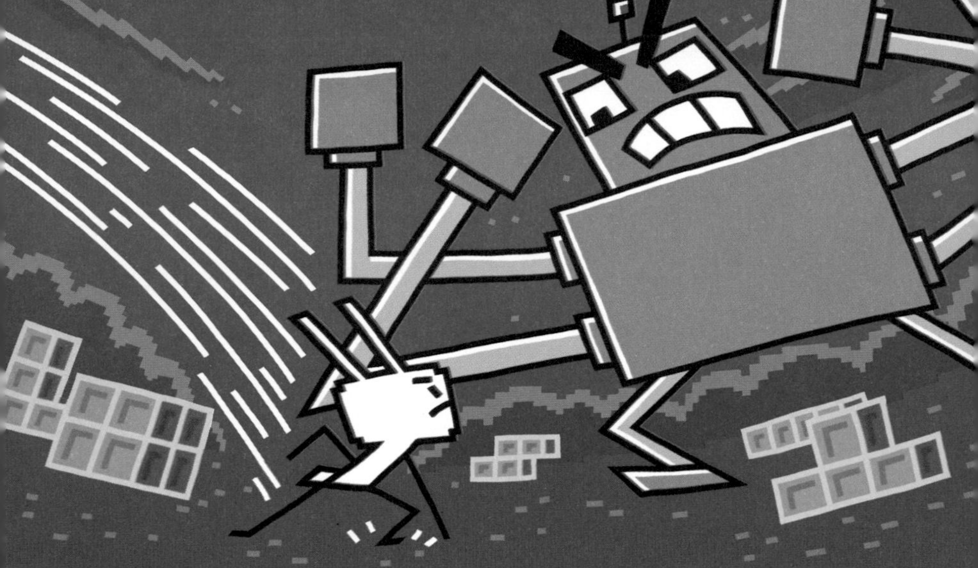

He travels from one robot attack . . .

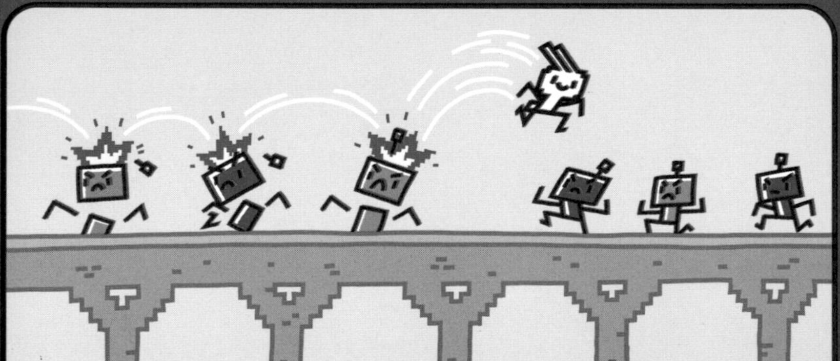

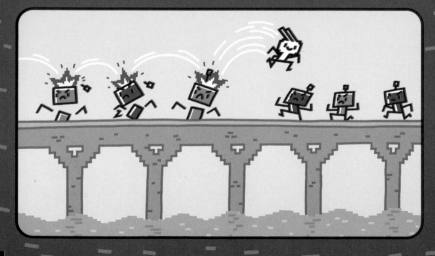

to another robot attack . . .

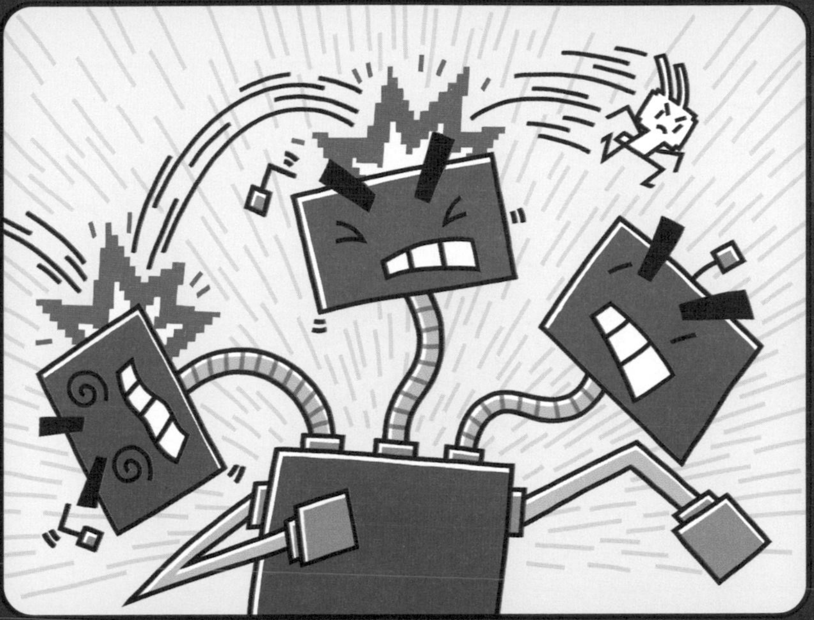

to yet another.

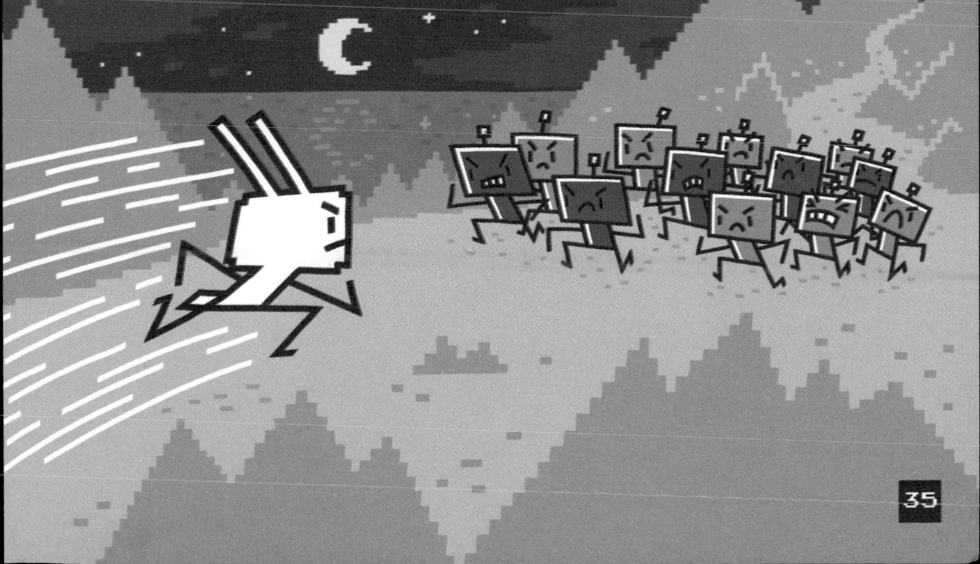

Super Rabbit Boy defeats every robot he finds.

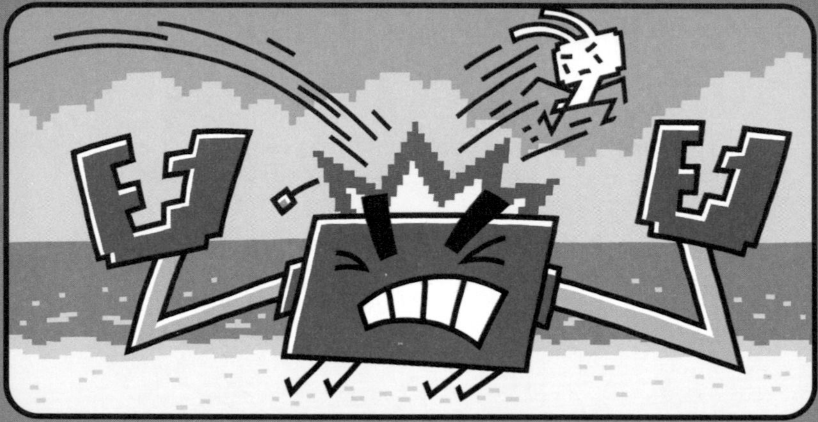

But Moon Girl keeps finding more.

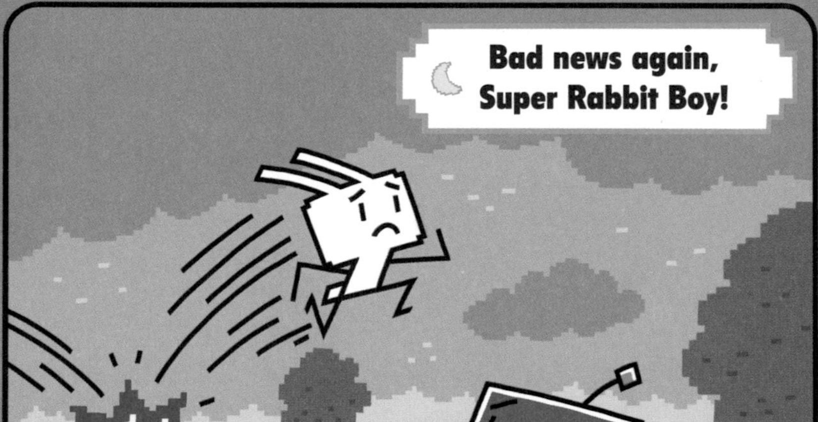
Bad news again, Super Rabbit Boy!

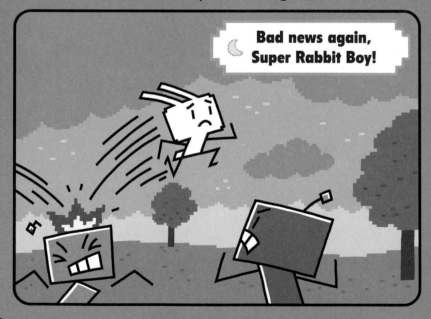

Super Rabbit Boy is getting tired.

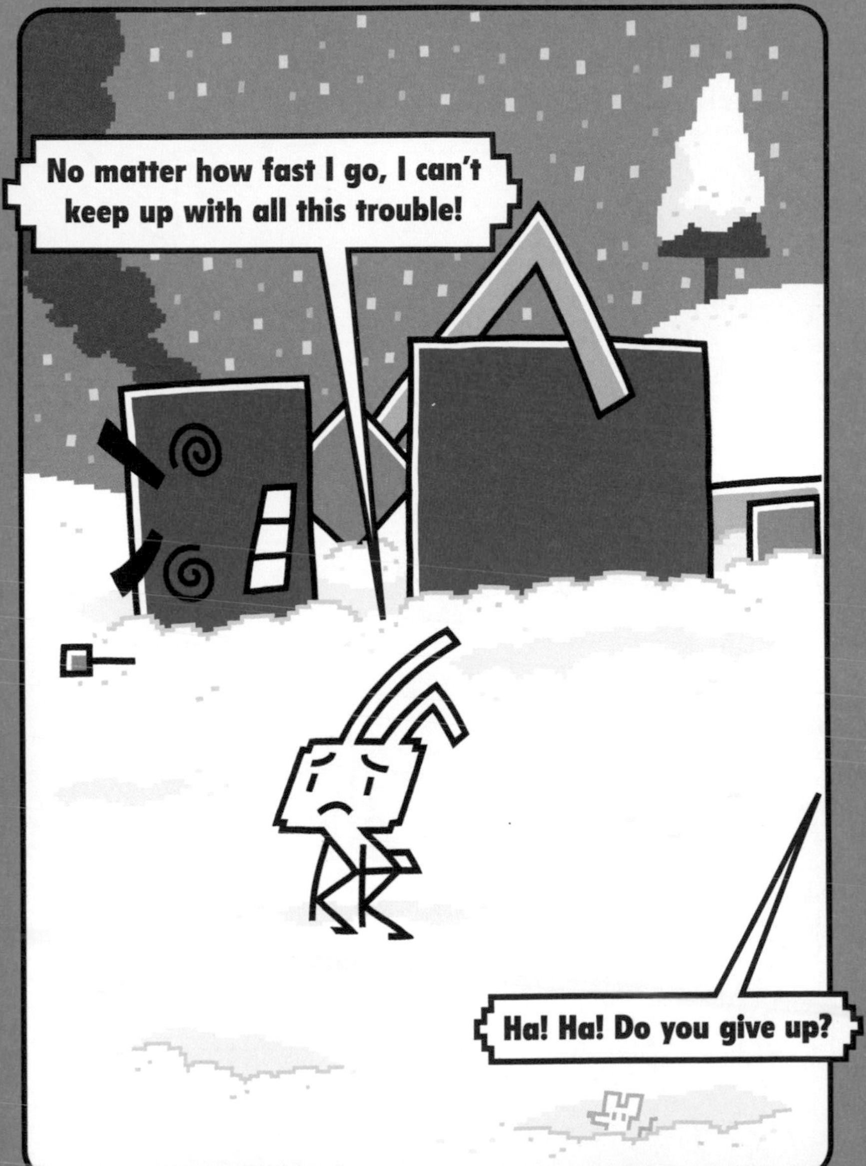
No matter how fast I go, I can't keep up with all this trouble!
Ha! Ha! Do you give up?

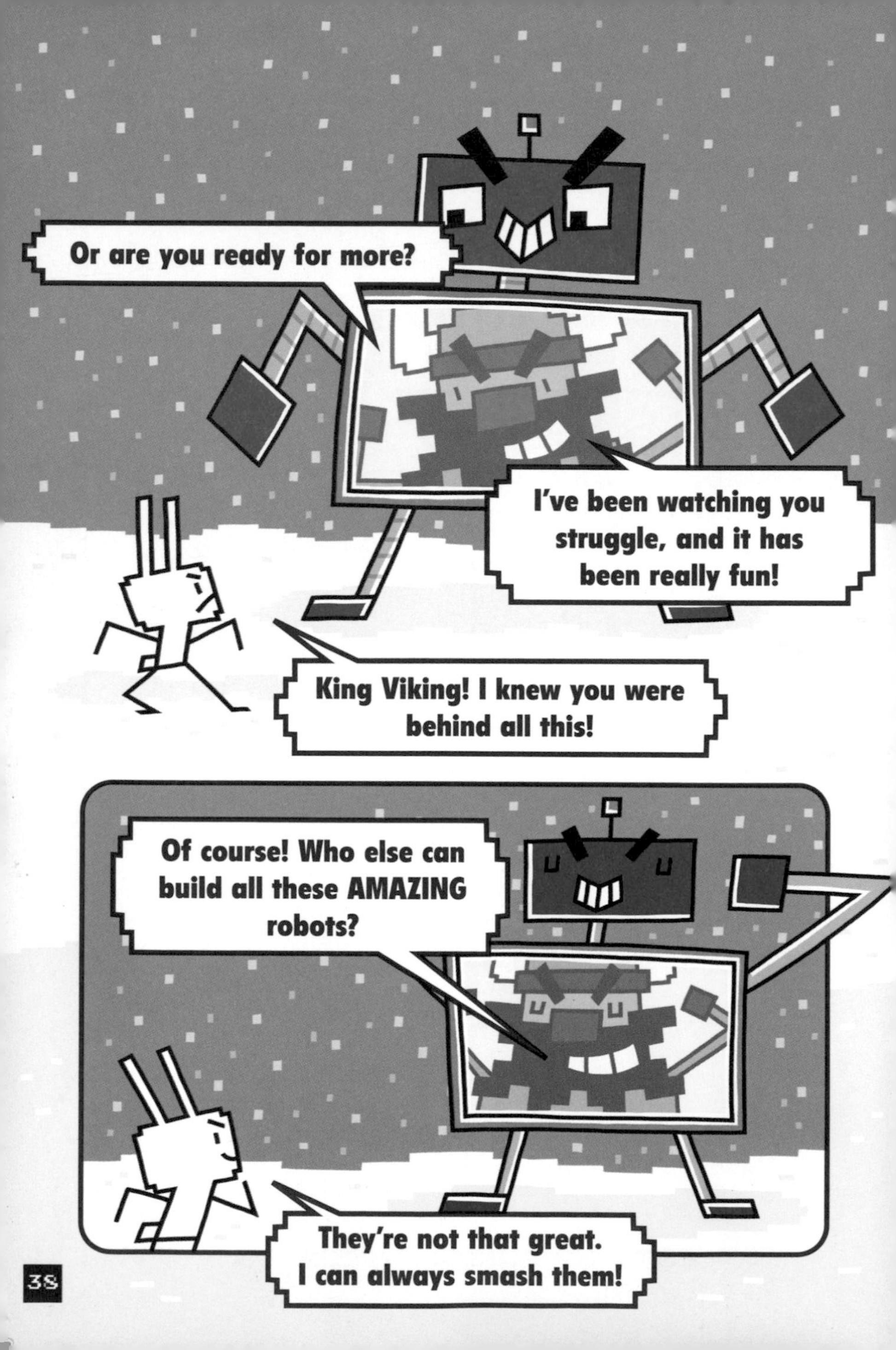
Or are you ready for more?
I've been watching you struggle, and it has been really fun!
King Viking! I knew you were behind all this!
Of course! Who else can build all these AMAZING robots?
They're not that great. I can always smash them!

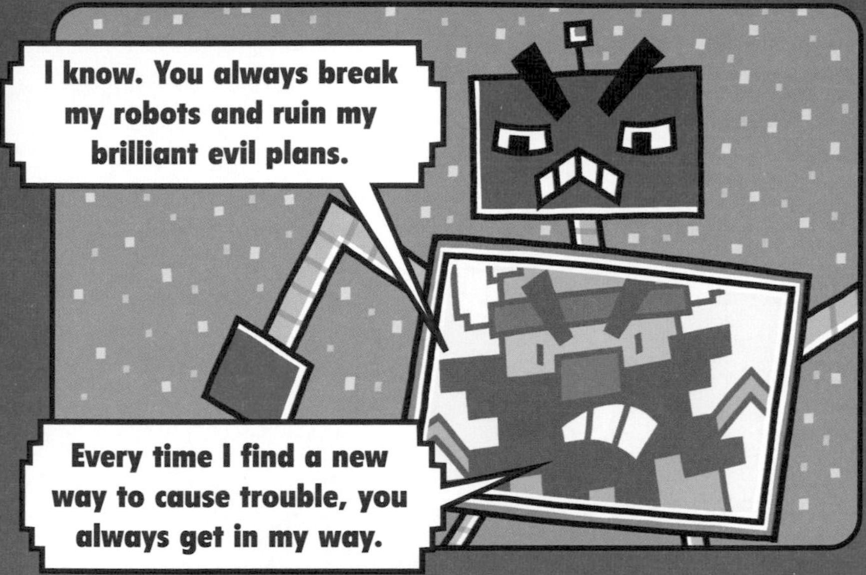
I know. You always break my robots and ruin my brilliant evil plans.
Every time I find a new way to cause trouble, you always get in my way.

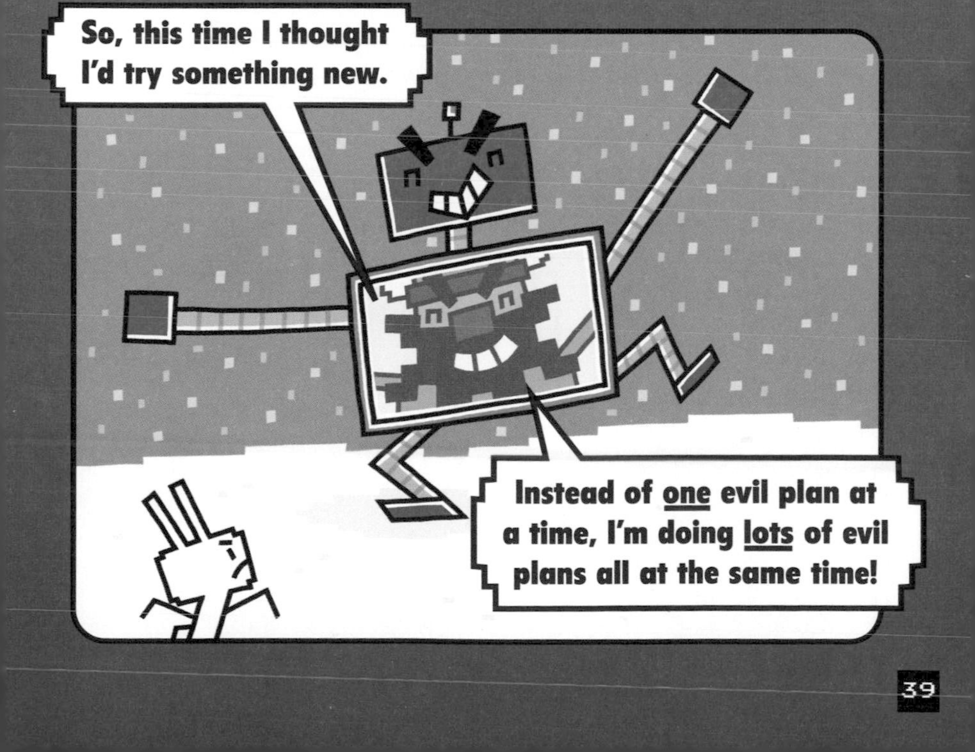
So, this time I thought I'd try something new.
Instead of one evil plan at a time, I'm doing lots of evil plans all at the same time!

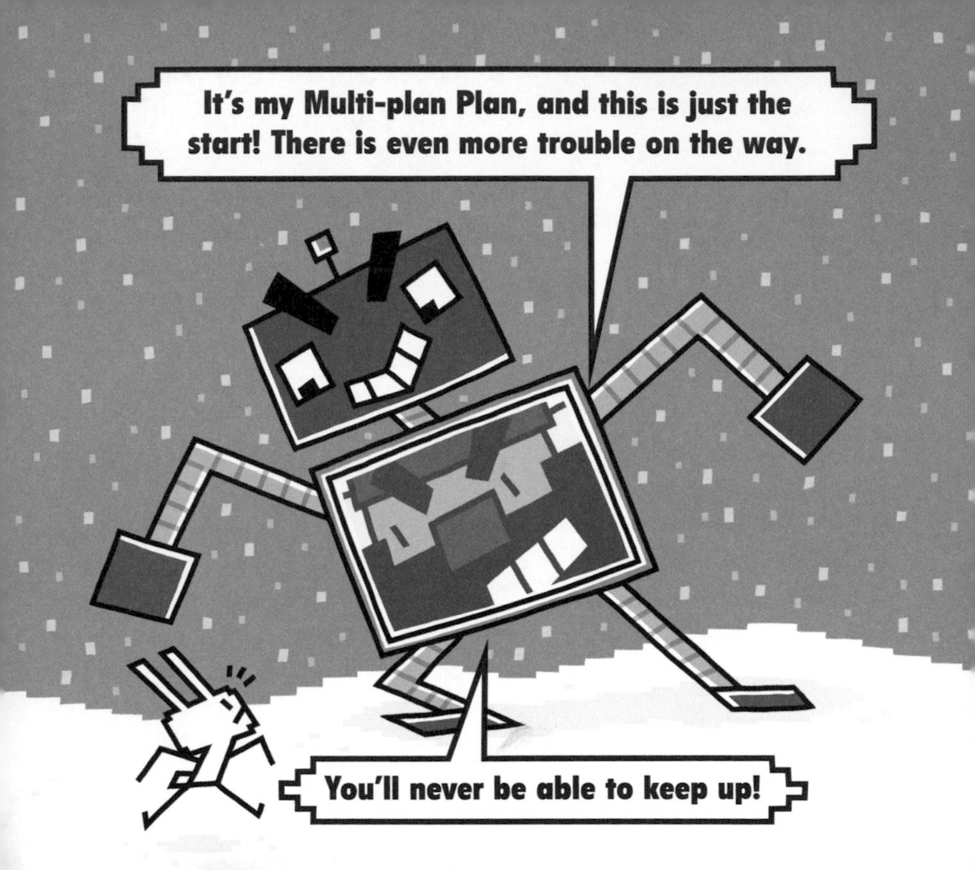
It's my Multi-plan Plan, and this is just the start! There is even more trouble on the way.
You'll never be able to keep up!

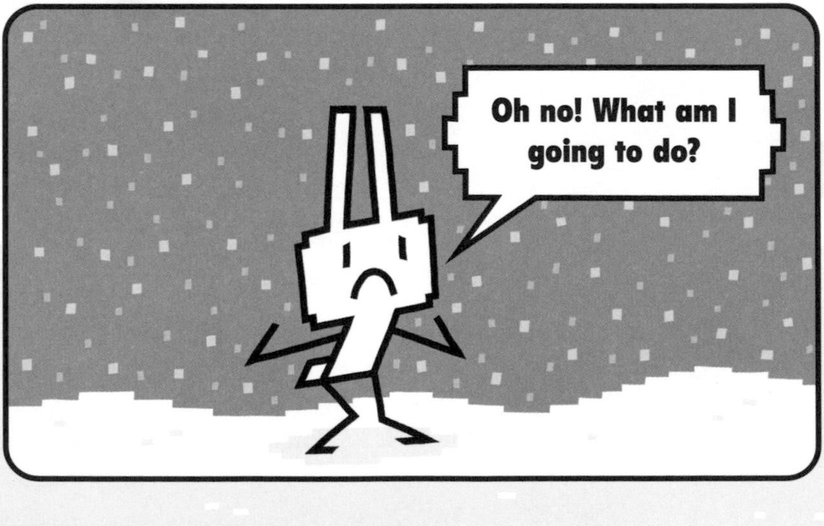
Oh no! What am I going to do?

7 BUSY BOY

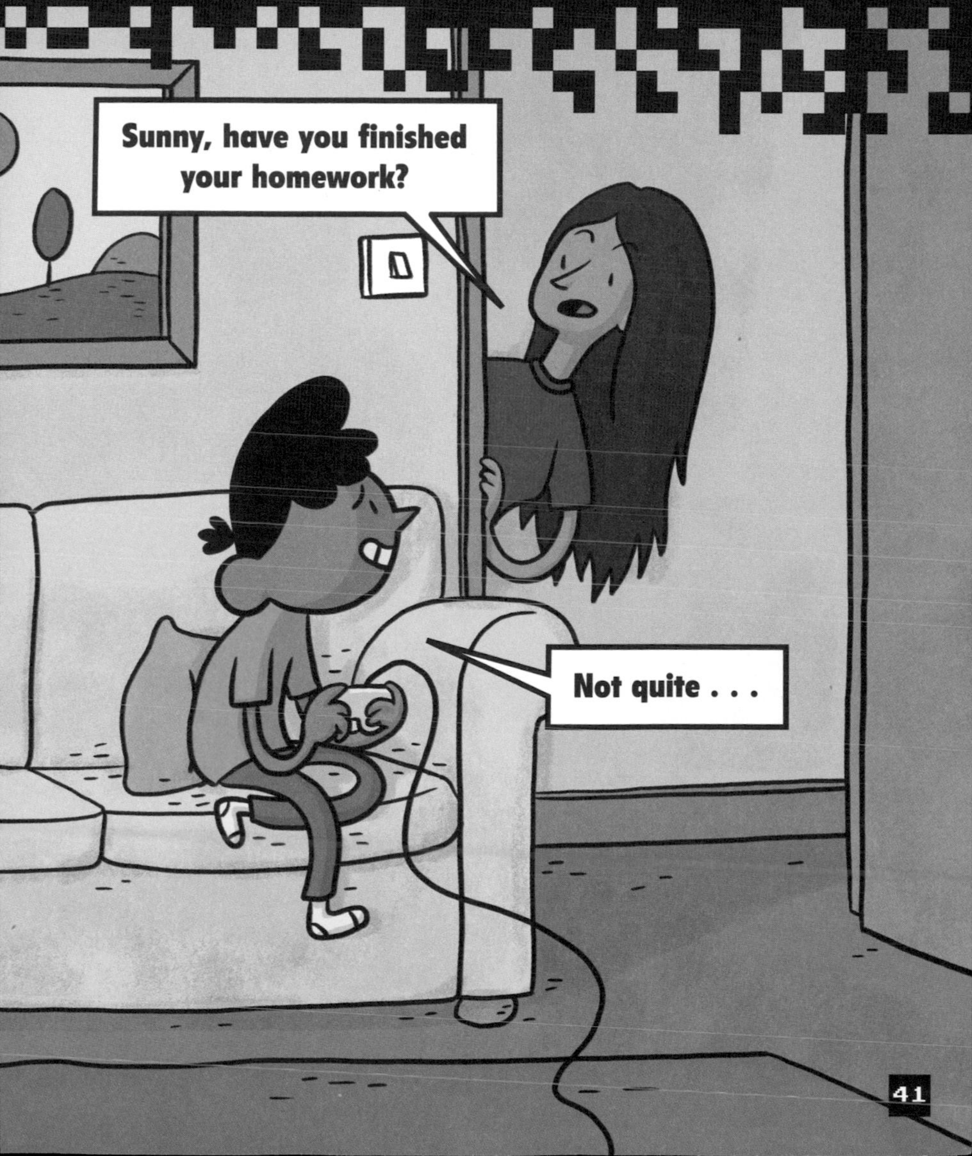
Sunny, have you finished your homework?
Not quite . . .

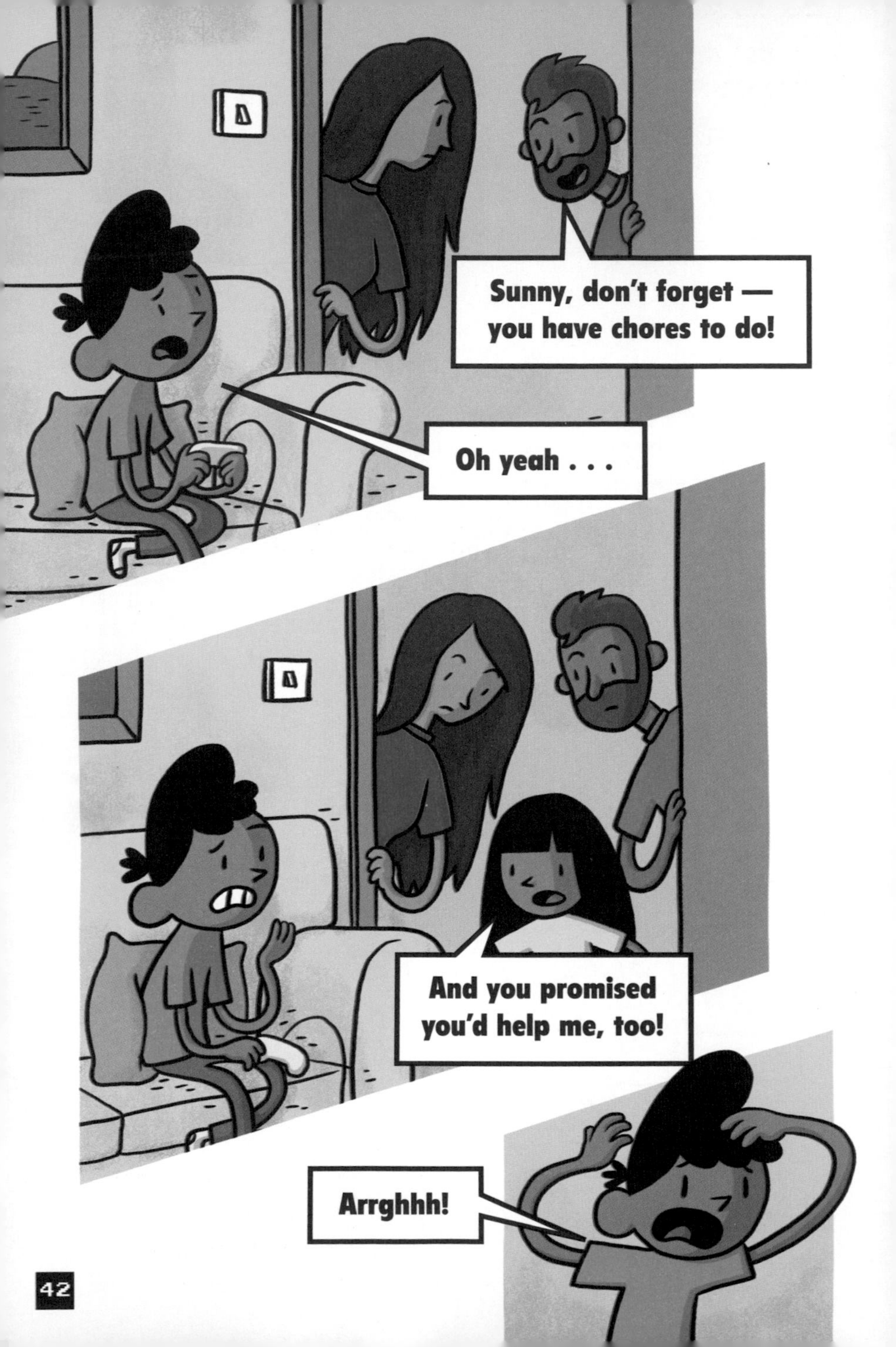
Sunny, don't forget — you have chores to do!
Oh yeah . . .
And you promised you'd help me, too!
Arrghhh!

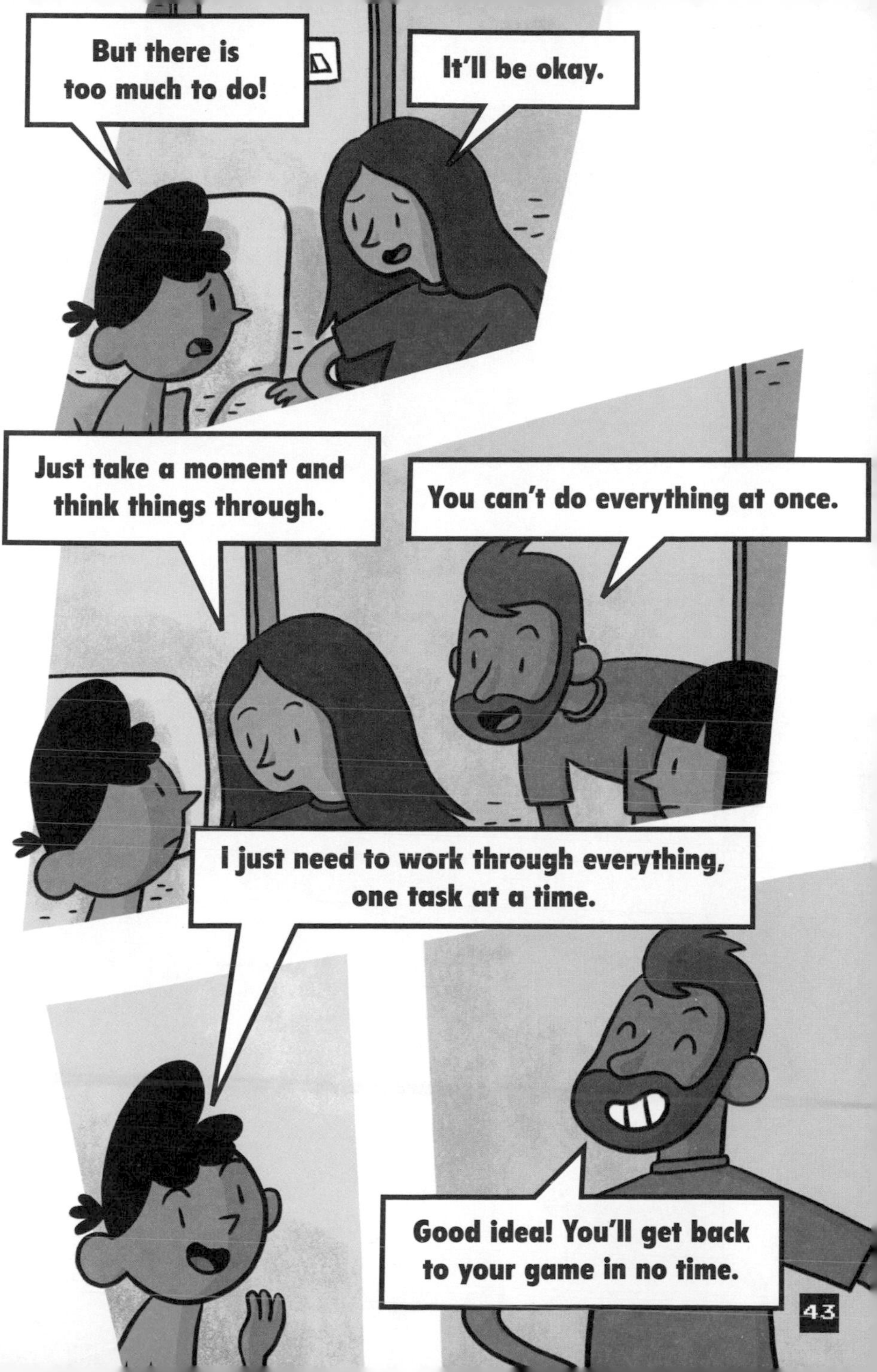

But there is too much to do!
It'll be okay.
Just take a moment and think things through.
You can't do everything at once.
I just need to work through everything, one task at a time.
Good idea! You'll get back to your game in no time.

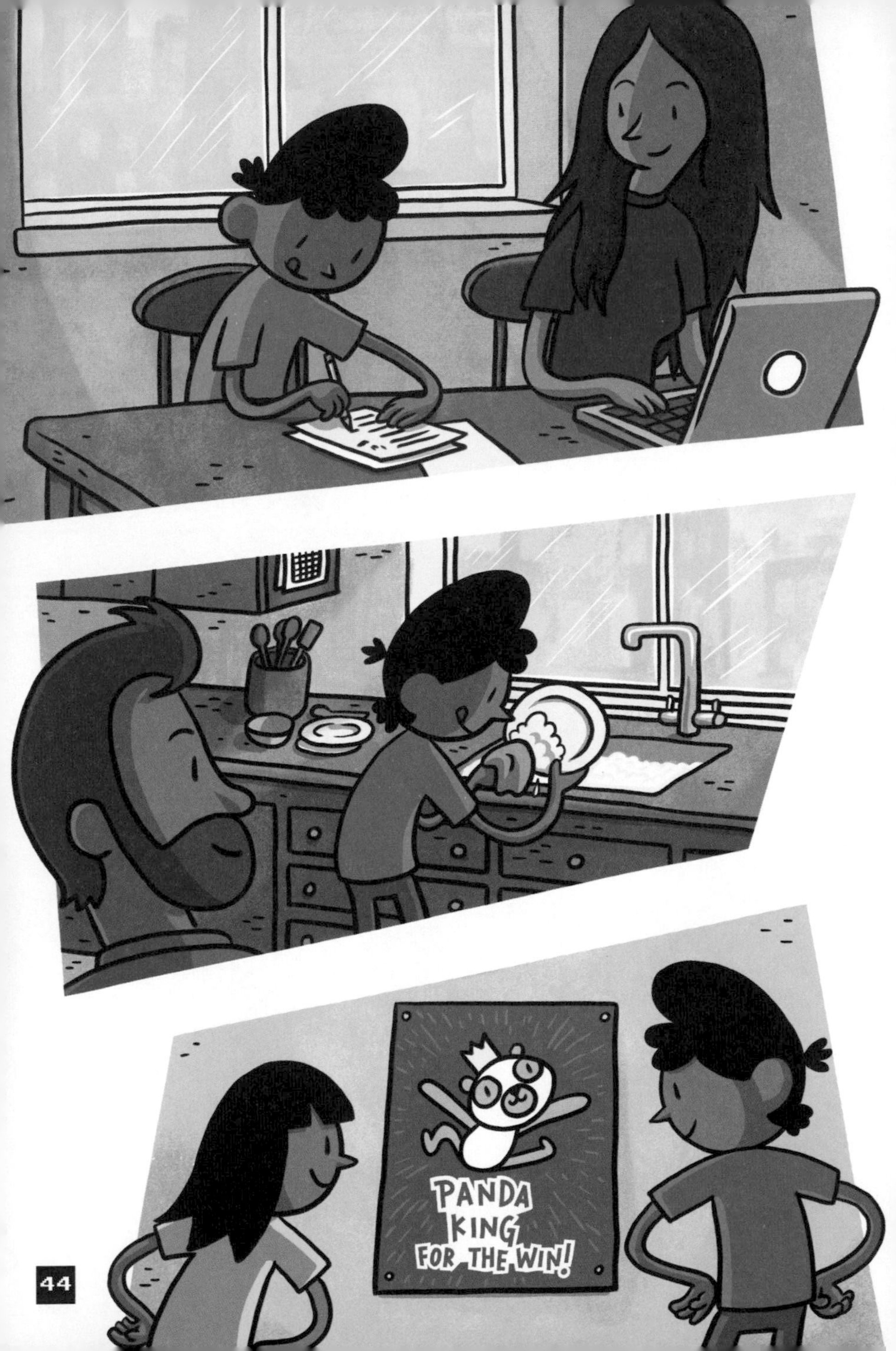
PANDA
KING
FOR THE WIN!

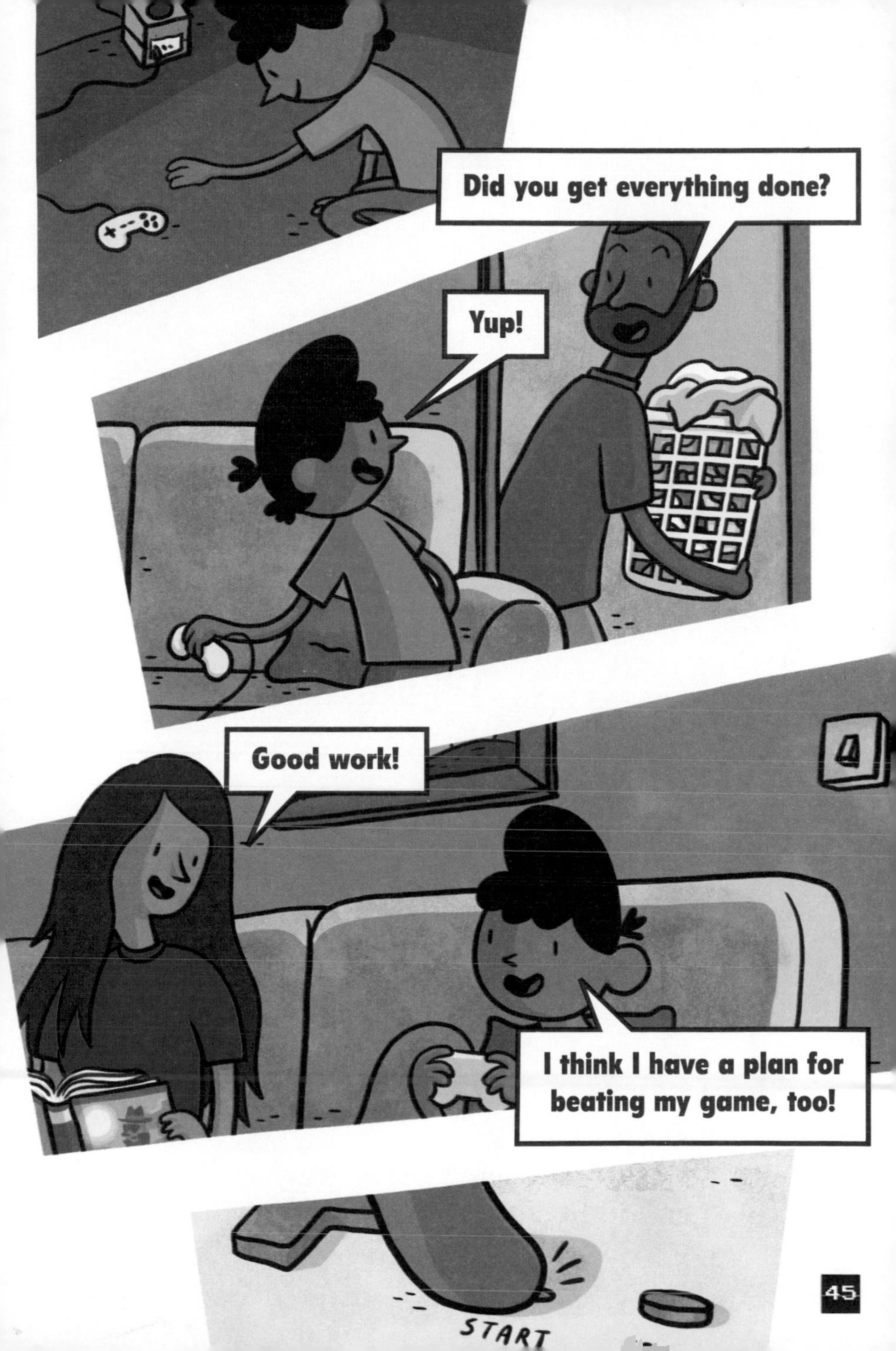
Did you get everything done?
Yup!
Good work!
I think I have a plan for beating my game, too!
START

8 A PLAN TO END ALL PLANS

Super Rabbit Boy won't give up. He's ready to take action!

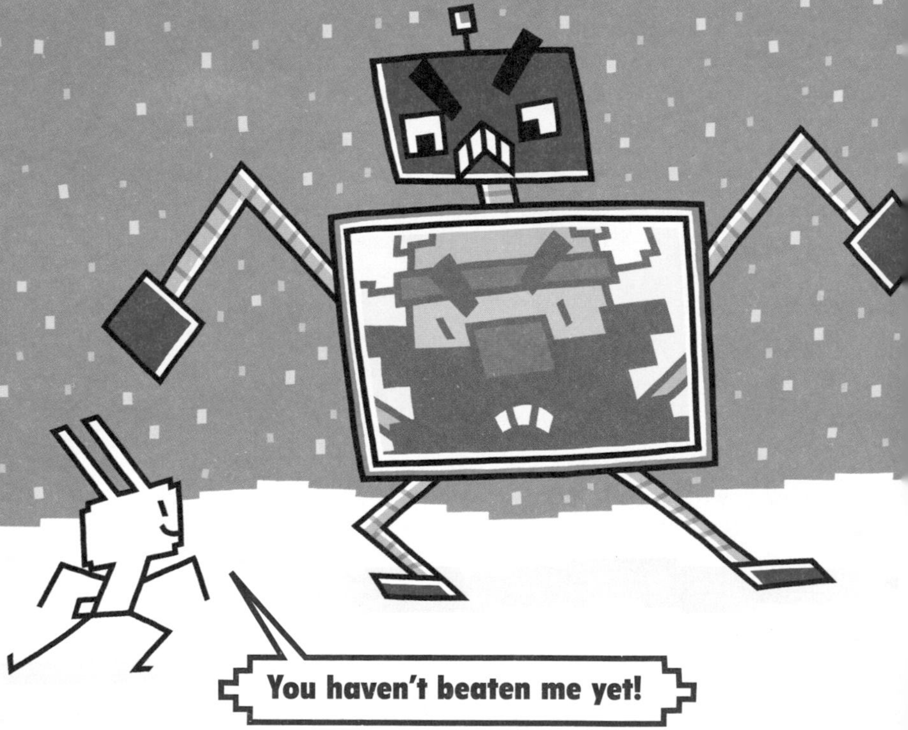
You haven't beaten me yet!

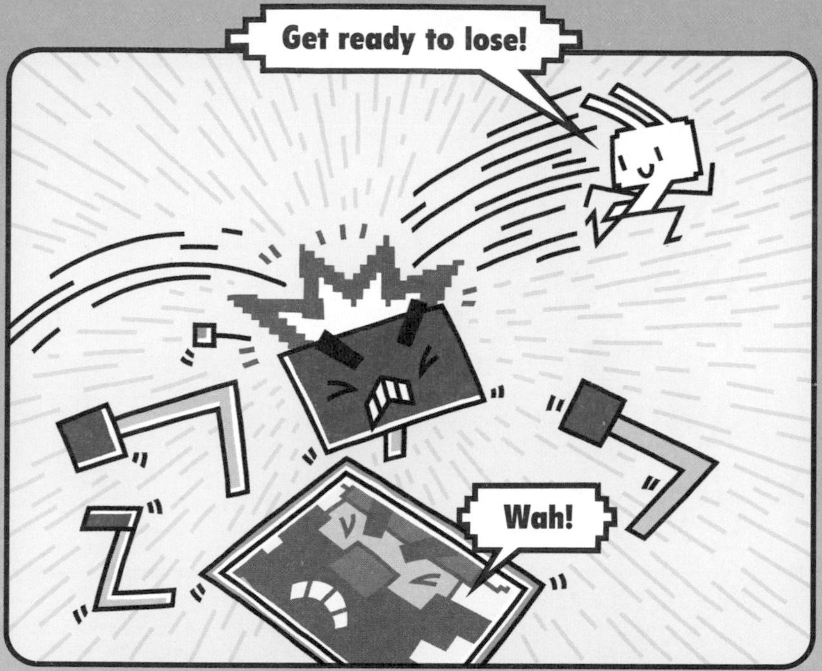
Get ready to lose!
Wah!

Super Rabbit Boy runs to a travel cannon nearby.

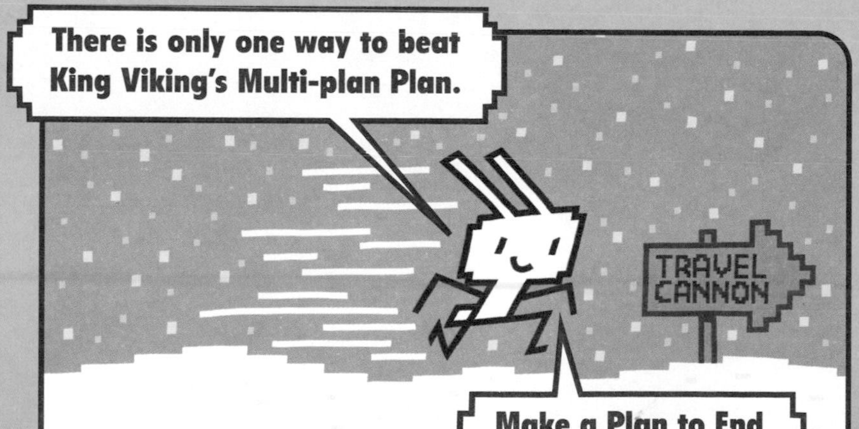
There is only one way to beat King Viking's Multi-plan Plan.
TRAVEL CANNON
Make a Plan to End All Plans!

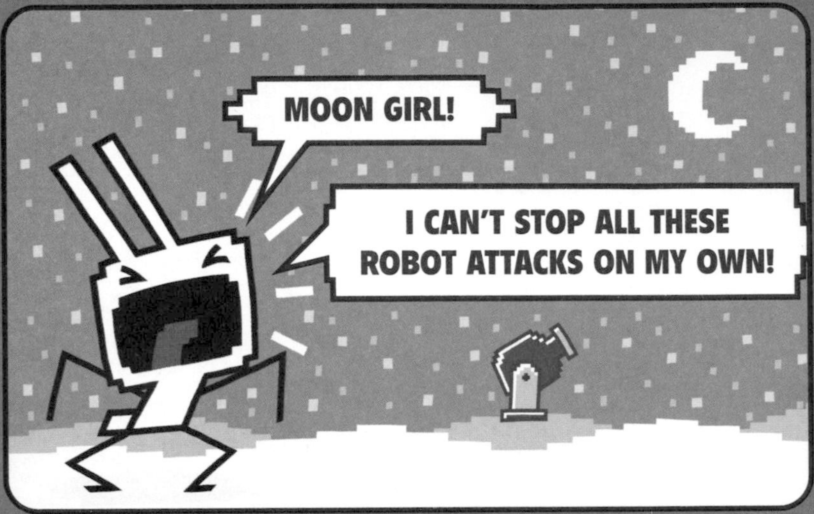
MOON GIRL!
I CAN'T STOP ALL THESE ROBOT ATTACKS ON MY OWN!

Moon Girl looks toward Super World. Super Rabbit Boy's voice is booming up from the planet!

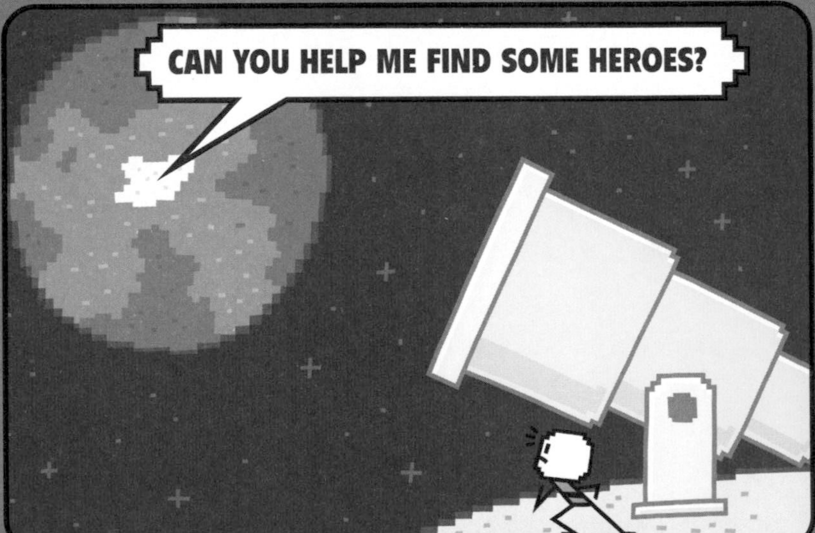
CAN YOU HELP ME FIND SOME HEROES?

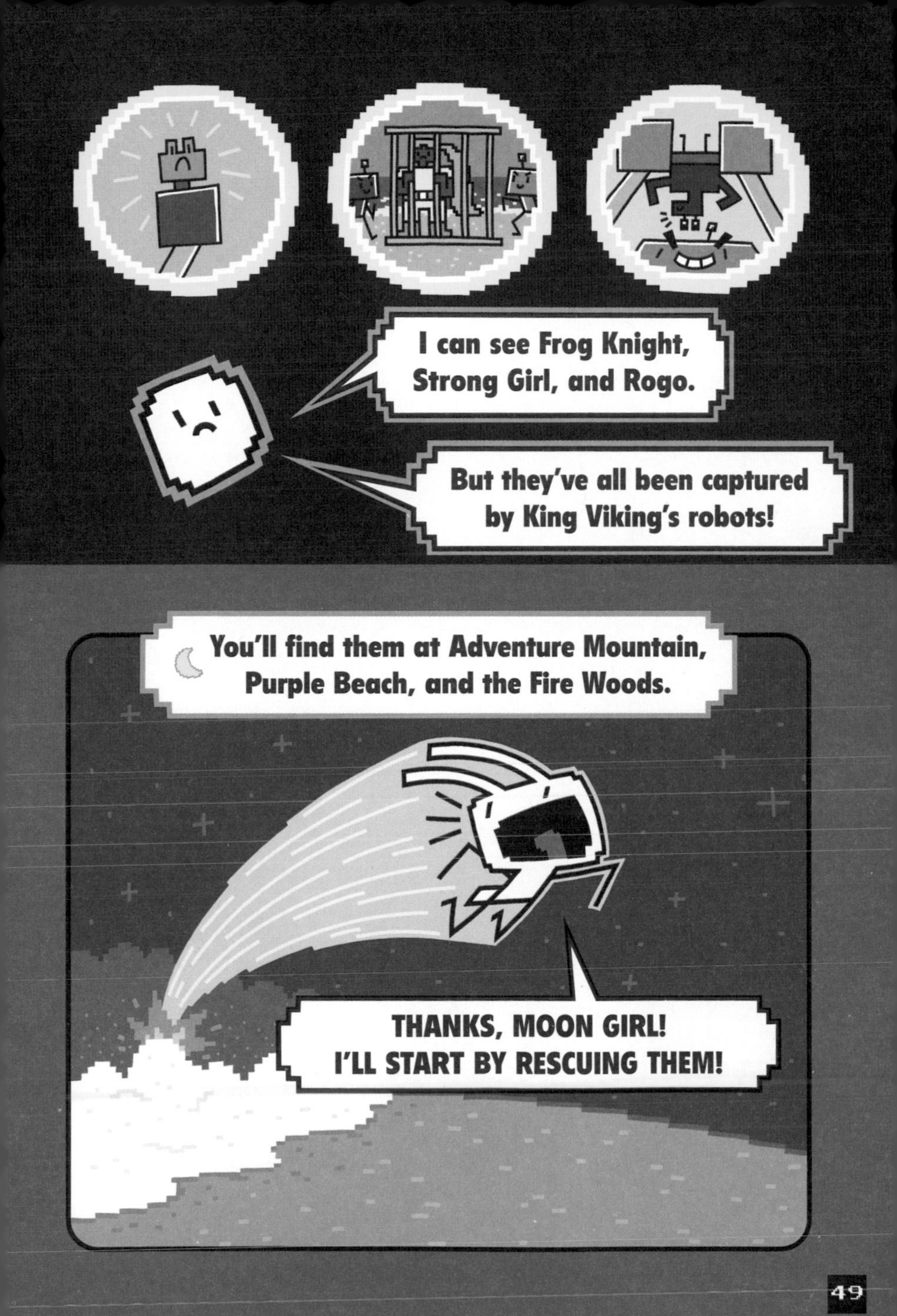
I can see Frog Knight, Strong Girl, and Rogo.
But they've all been captured by King Viking's robots!
You'll find them at Adventure Mountain, Purple Beach, and the Fire Woods.
THANKS, MOON GIRL! I'LL START BY RESCUING THEM!

First, Super Rabbit Boy rescues Frog Knight.

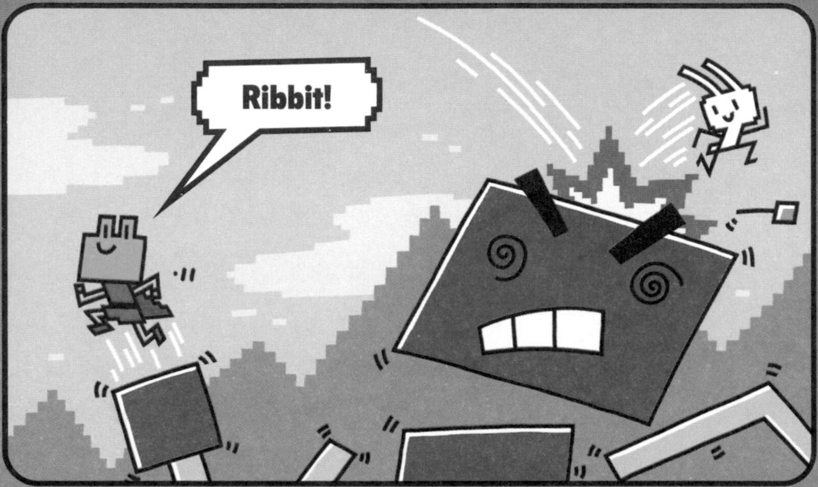
Ribbit!

Then Frog Knight frees Strong Girl.

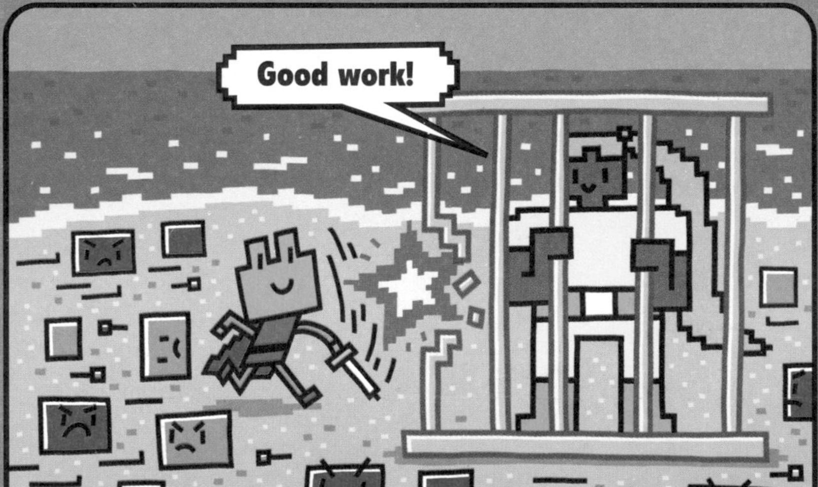
Good work!

Meanwhile, Super Rabbit Boy saves Rogo.

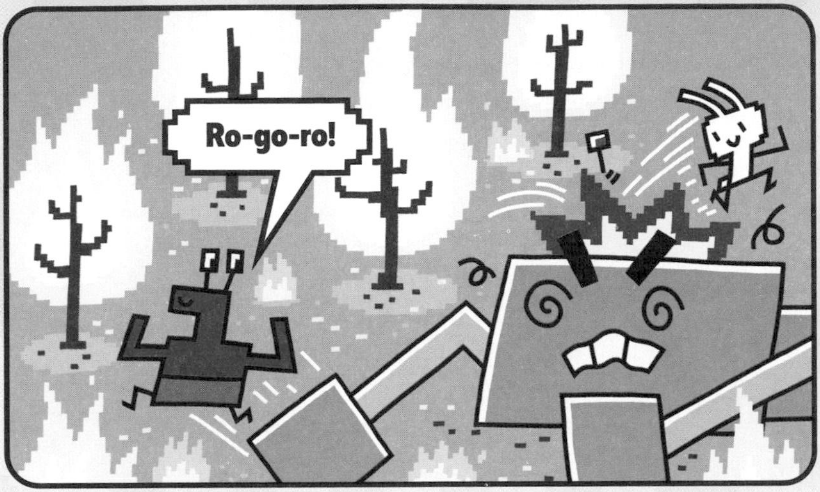

Ro-go-ro!

Super Rabbit Boy has found some help at last.

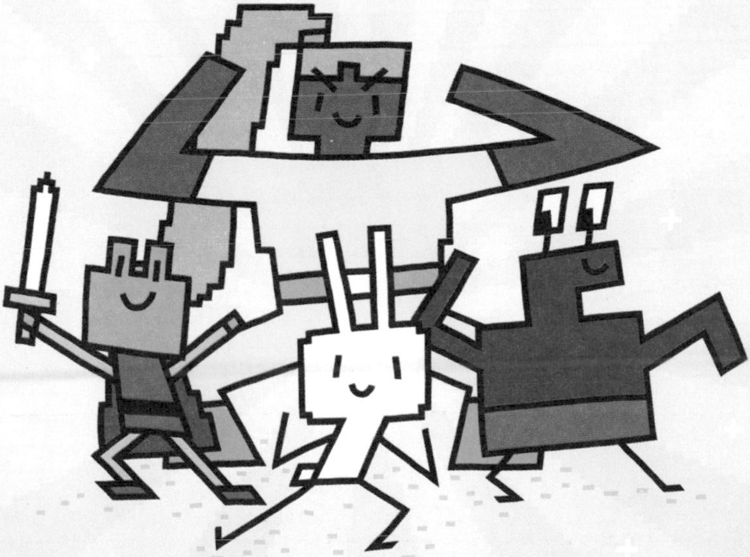

Super Rabbit Boy tells the other heroes about King Viking's Multi-plan Plan. Then he tells them his Plan to End All Plans.

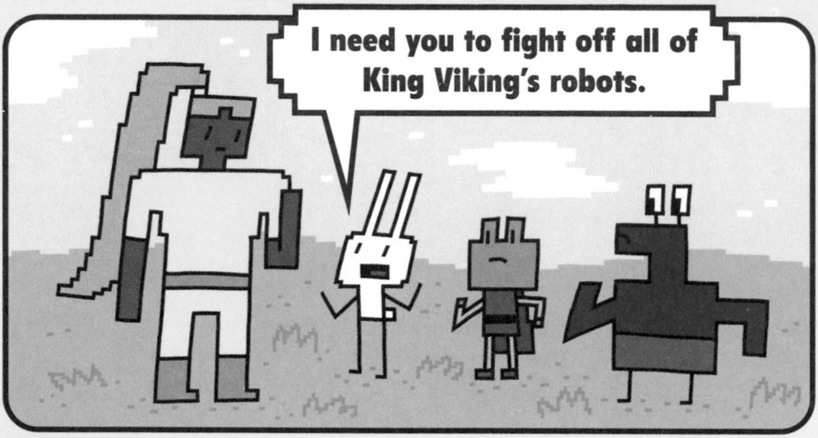
I need you to fight off all of King Viking's robots.

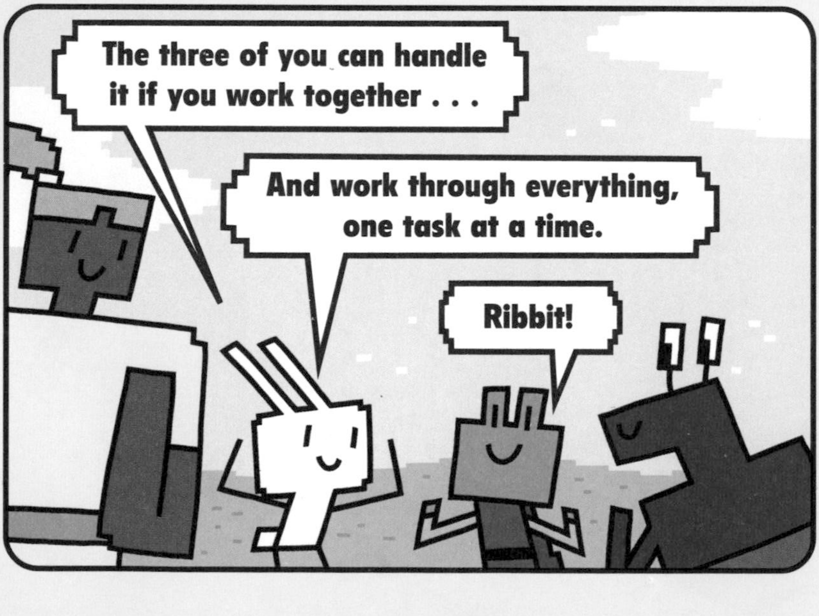
The three of you can handle it if you work together . . .
And work through everything, one task at a time.
Ribbit!

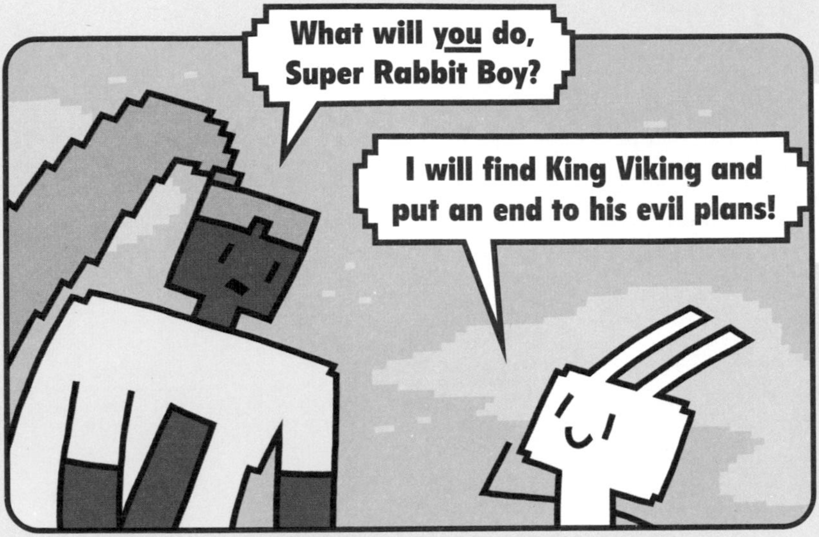
What will you do, Super Rabbit Boy?
I will find King Viking and put an end to his evil plans!

Super Rabbit Boy blasts off in search of King Viking. Where could that meanie be hiding?

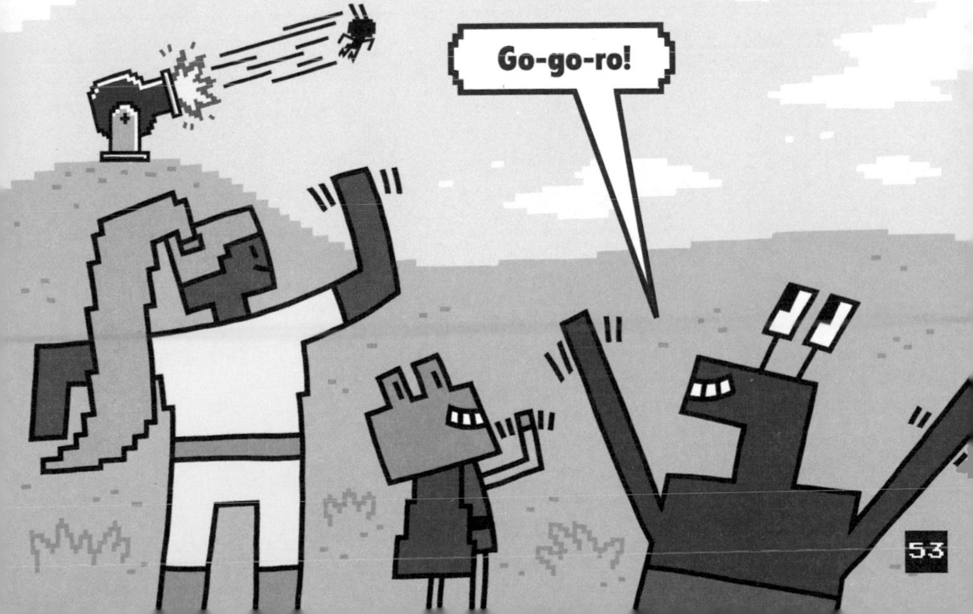
Go-go-ro!

9 HIDE-AND-SEEK

Super Rabbit Boy is back on the moon.

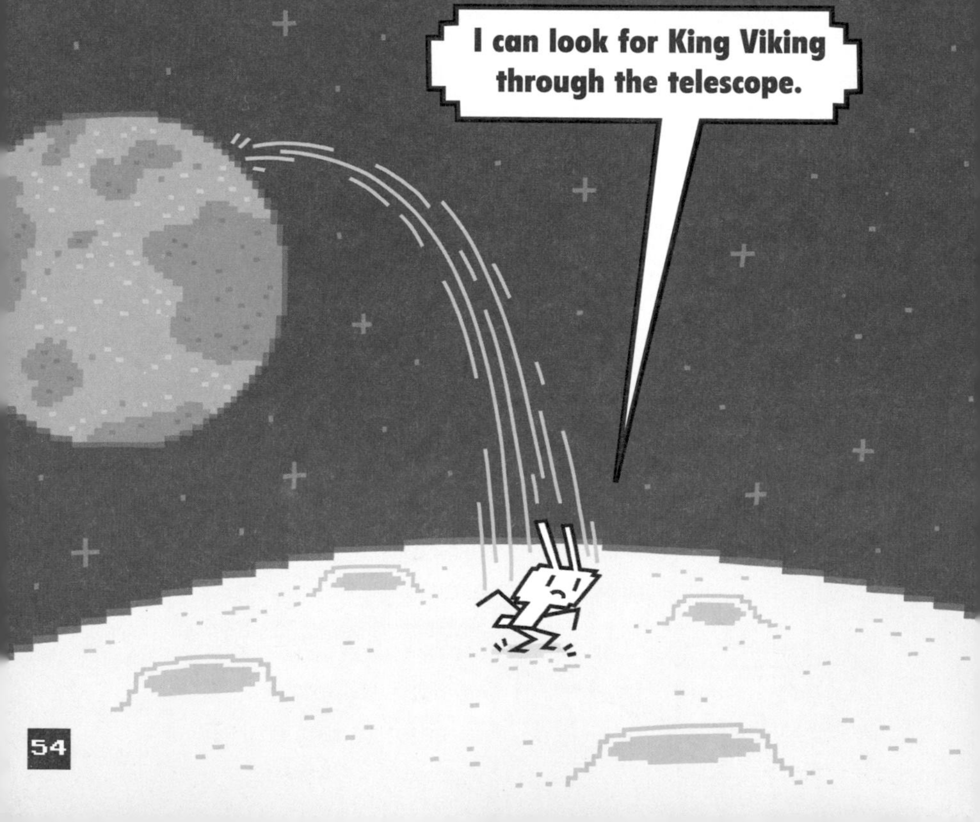
I can look for King Viking through the telescope.

Moon Girl has some news for him.

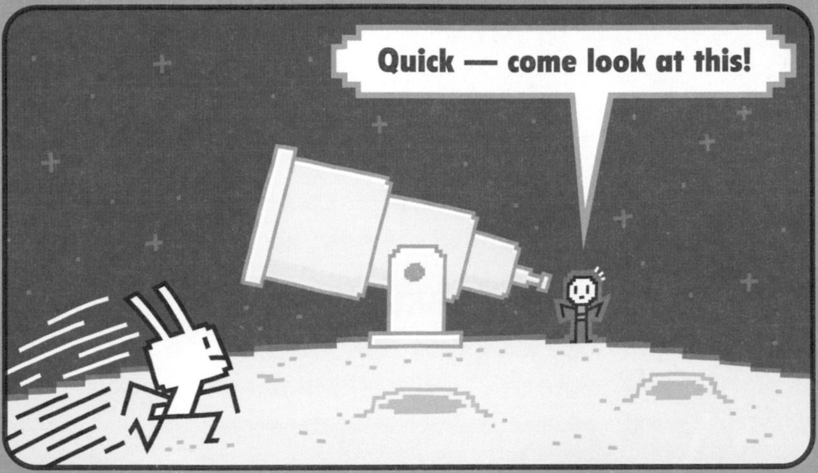
Quick — come look at this!

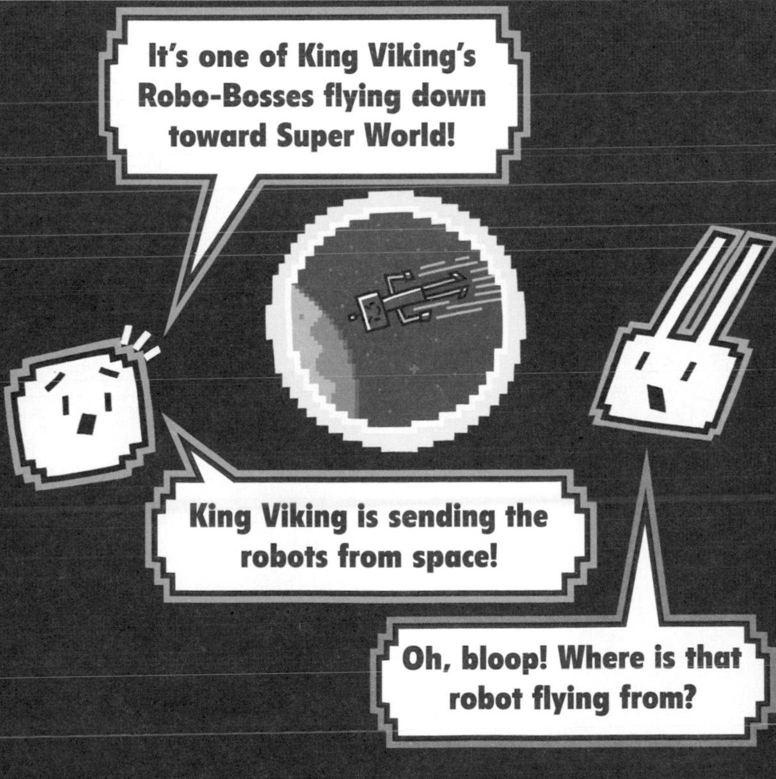
It's one of King Viking's Robo-Bosses flying down toward Super World!
King Viking is sending the robots from space!
Oh, bloop! Where is that robot flying from?

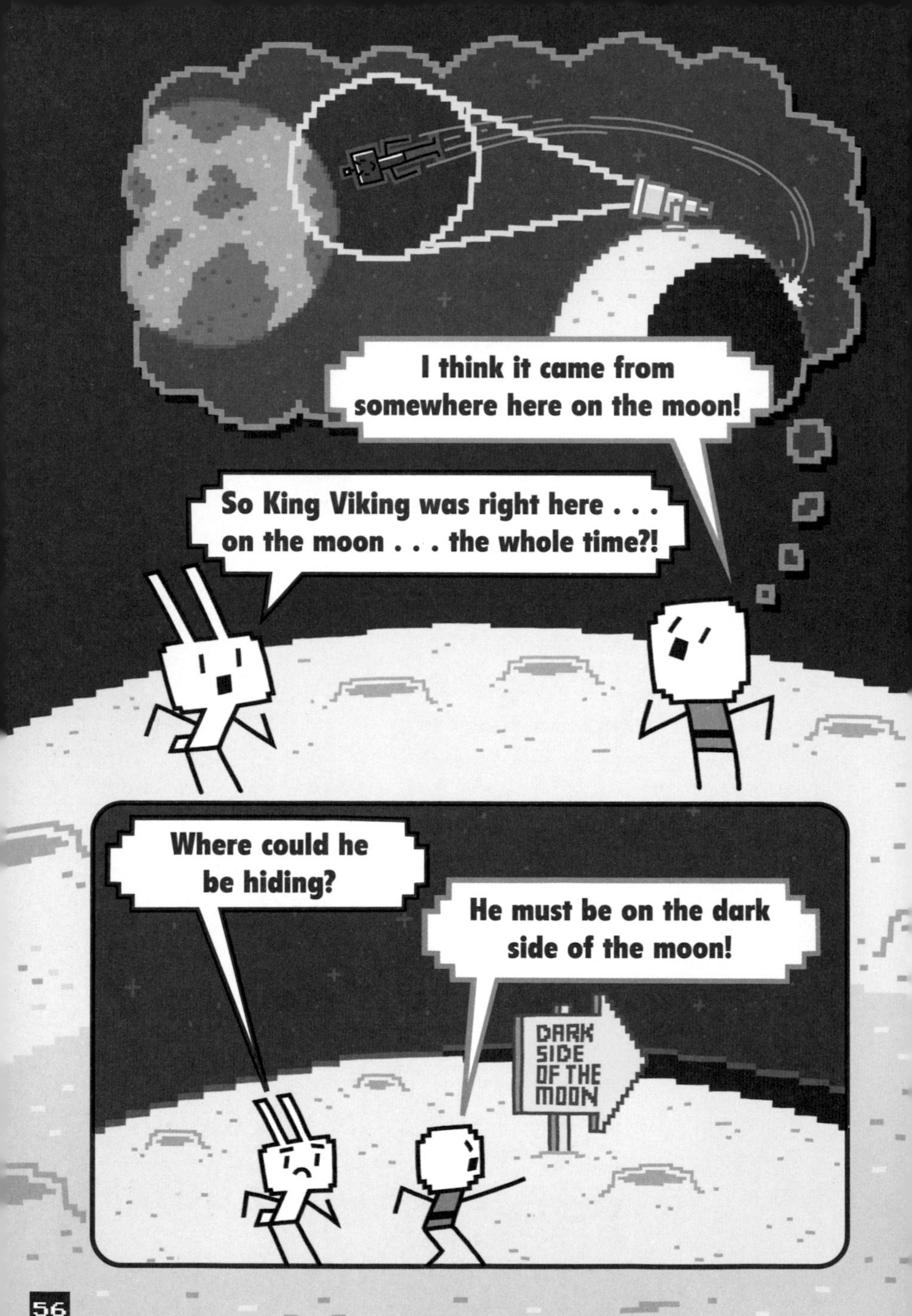
I think it came from somewhere here on the moon!
So King Viking was right here . . . on the moon . . . the whole time?!
Where could he be hiding?
He must be on the dark side of the moon!
DARK SIDE OF THE MOON

Super Rabbit Boy sets off in search of King Viking.

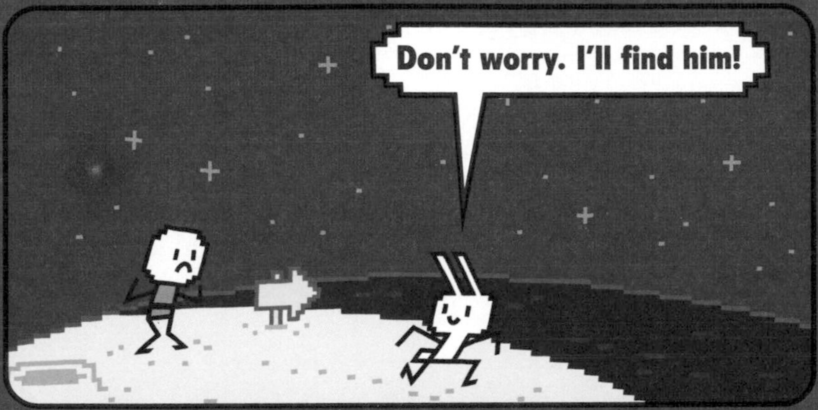
Don't worry. I'll find him!

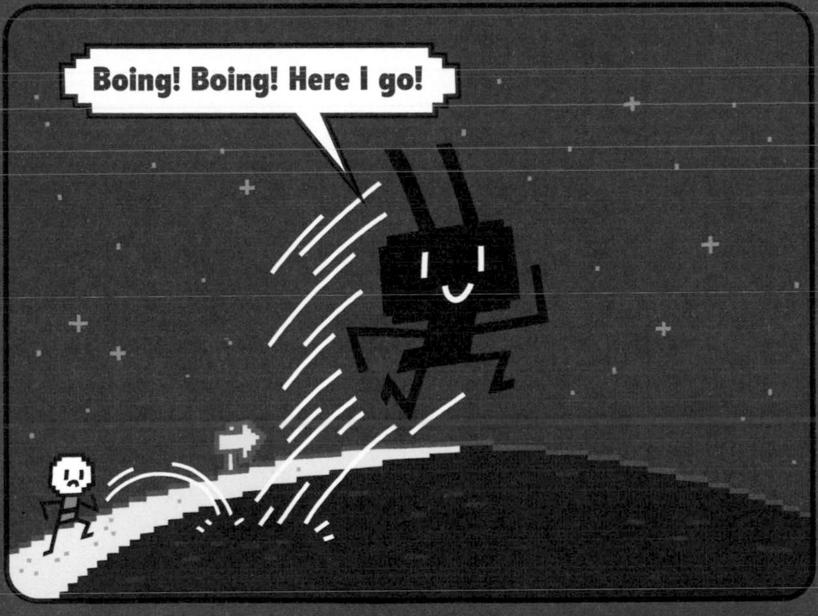
Boing! Boing! Here I go!

Super Rabbit Boy is surrounded by darkness.

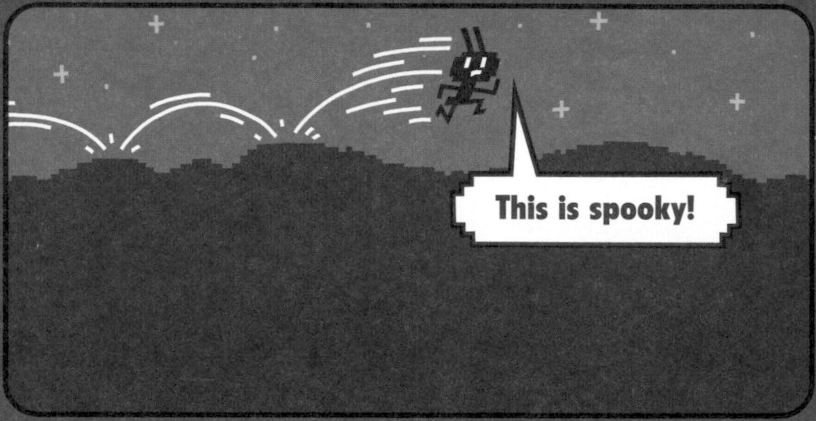
This is spooky!

It's hard to see anything. Super Rabbit Boy stumbles around as he searches.

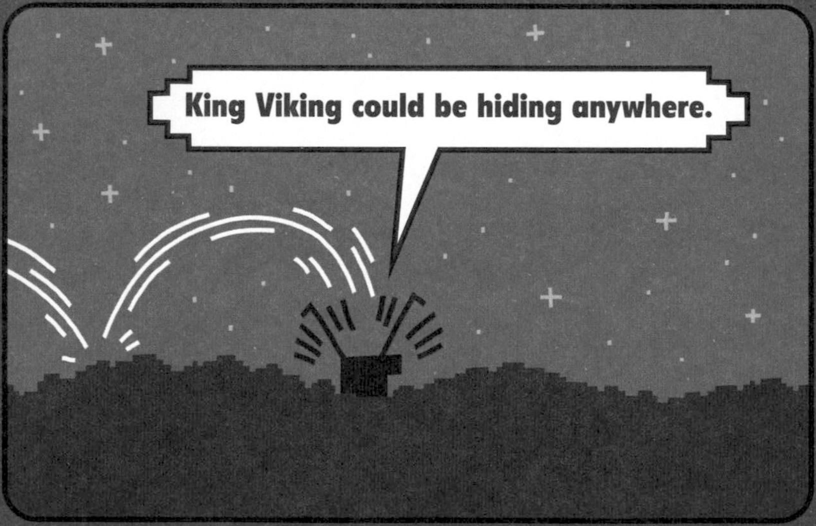
King Viking could be hiding anywhere.

He keeps searching through the darkness. He finally spots a glow coming from a crater.

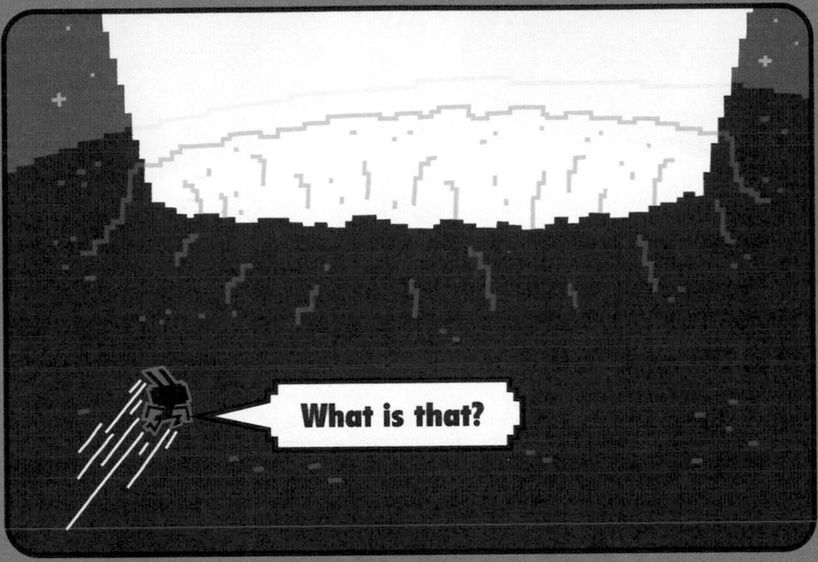
What is that?

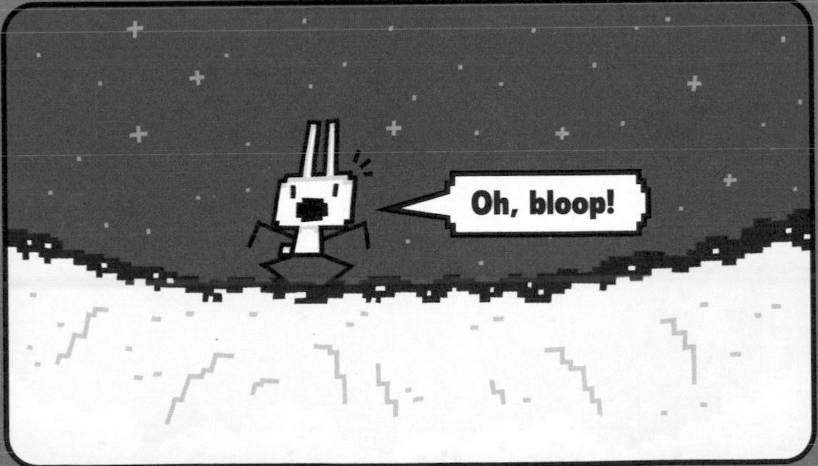
Oh, bloop!

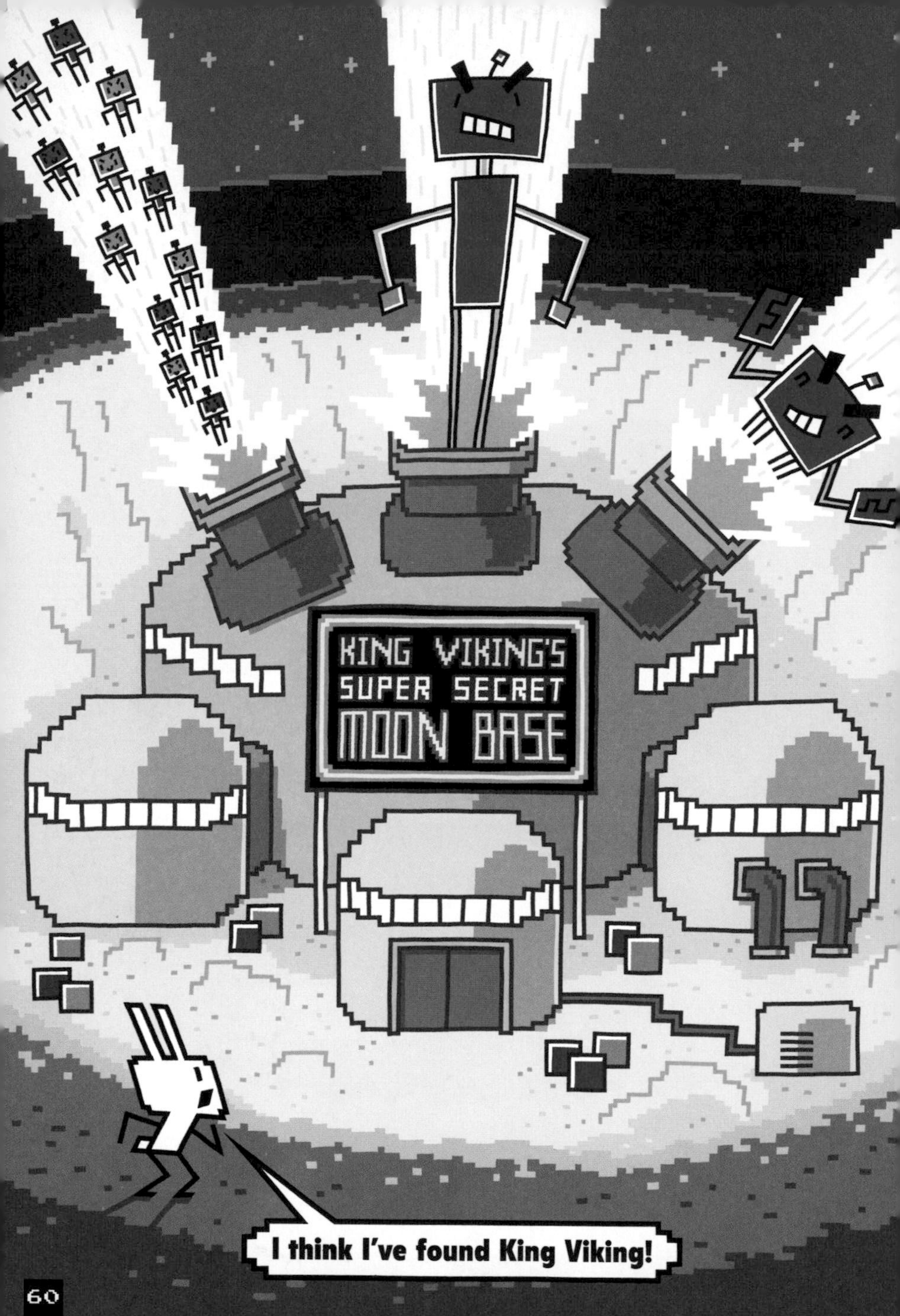
KING VIKING'S
SUPER SECRET
MOON BASE
I think I've found King Viking!

10 PRACTICE MAKES PERFECT

Super Rabbit Boy makes his way to the front door of King Viking's moon base.

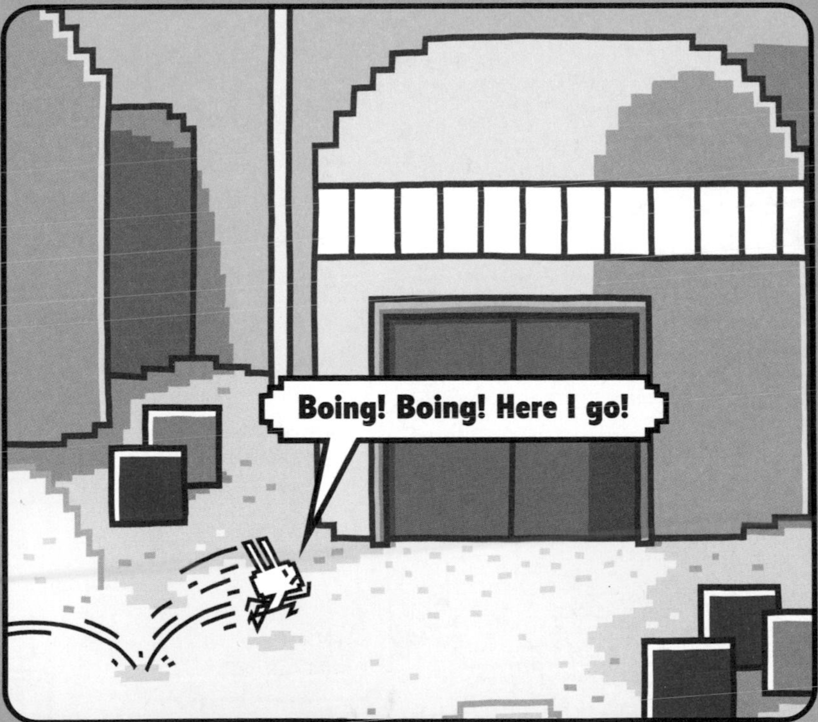
Boing! Boing! Here I go!

He has found King Viking and a giant robot-building machine. King Viking is making lots of robots, and then blasting them down to Super World!

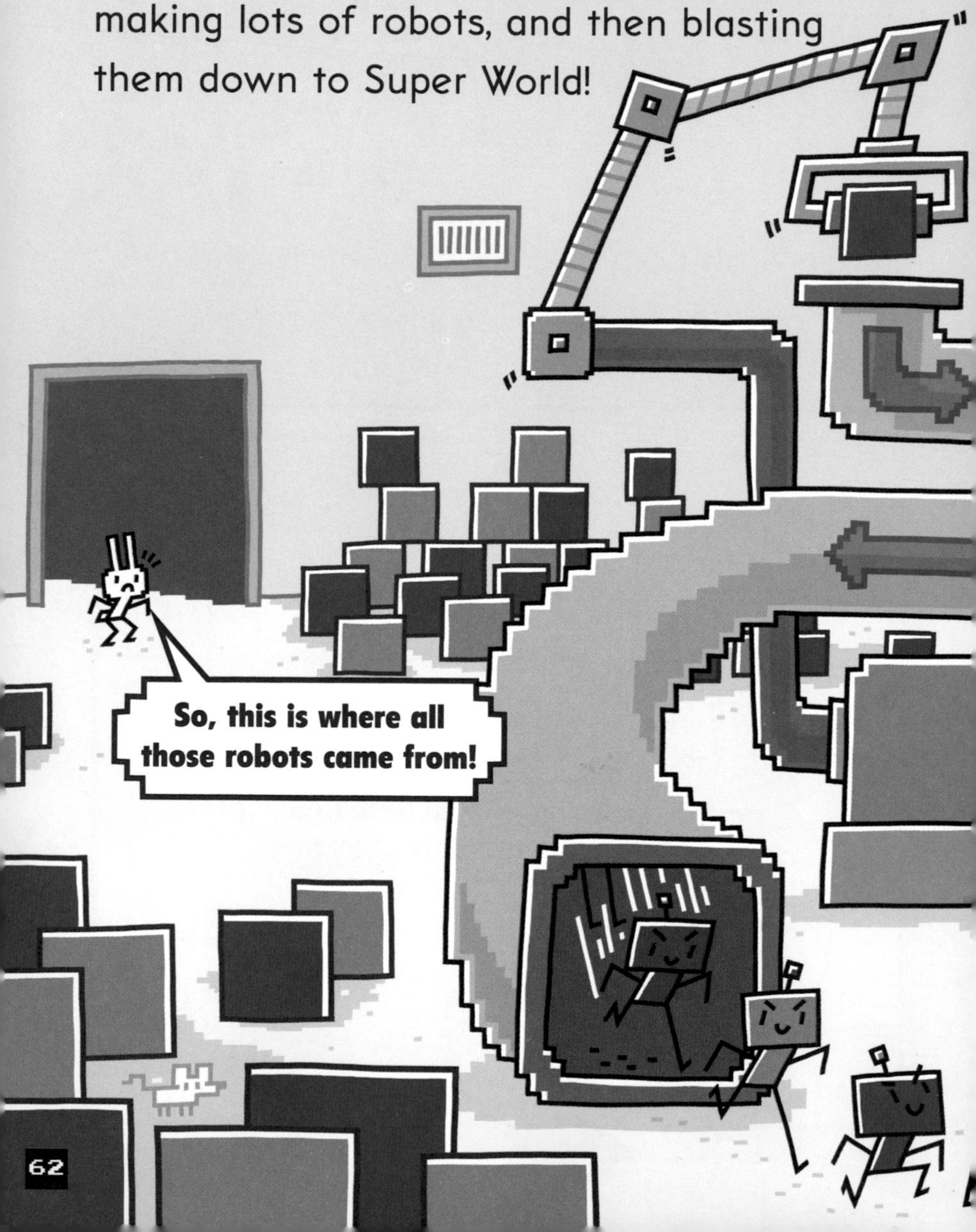
So, this is where all those robots came from!

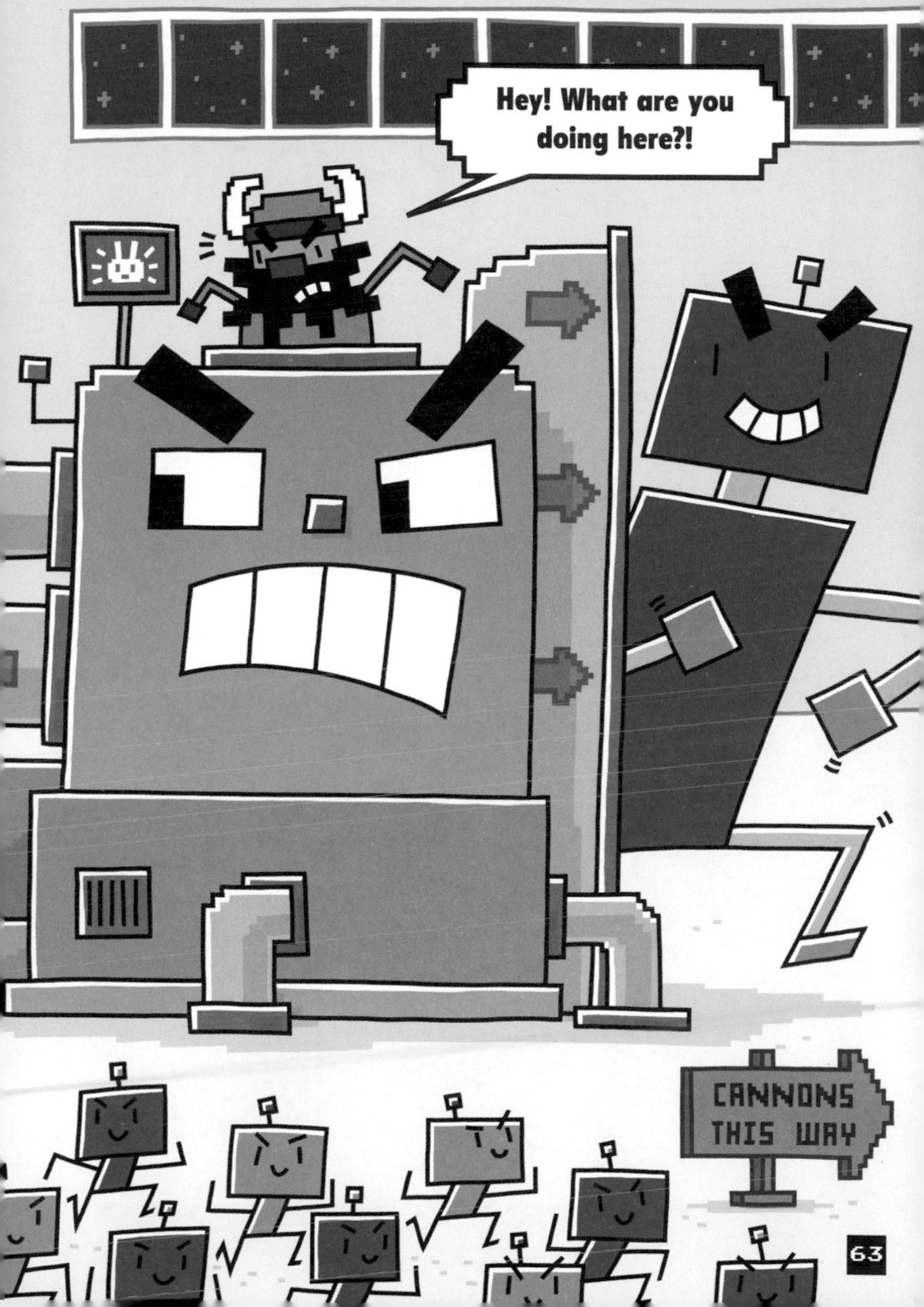
Hey! What are you doing here?!
CANNONS THIS WAY

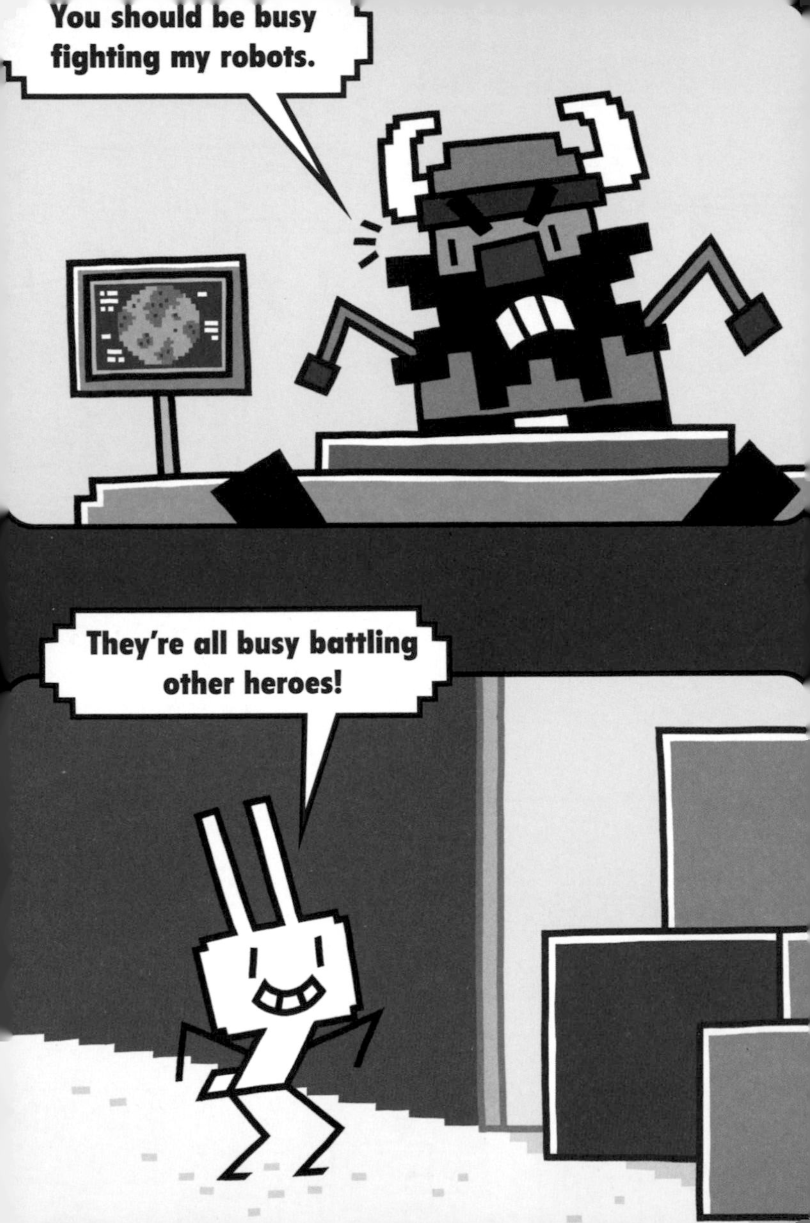
You should be busy fighting my robots.
They're all busy battling other heroes!

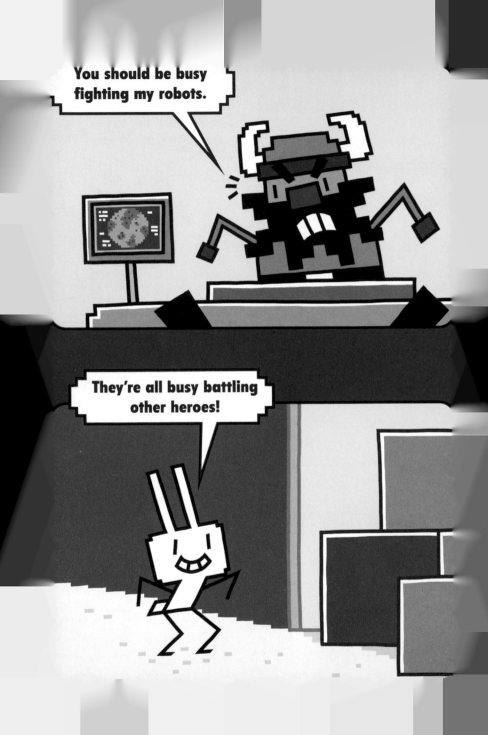

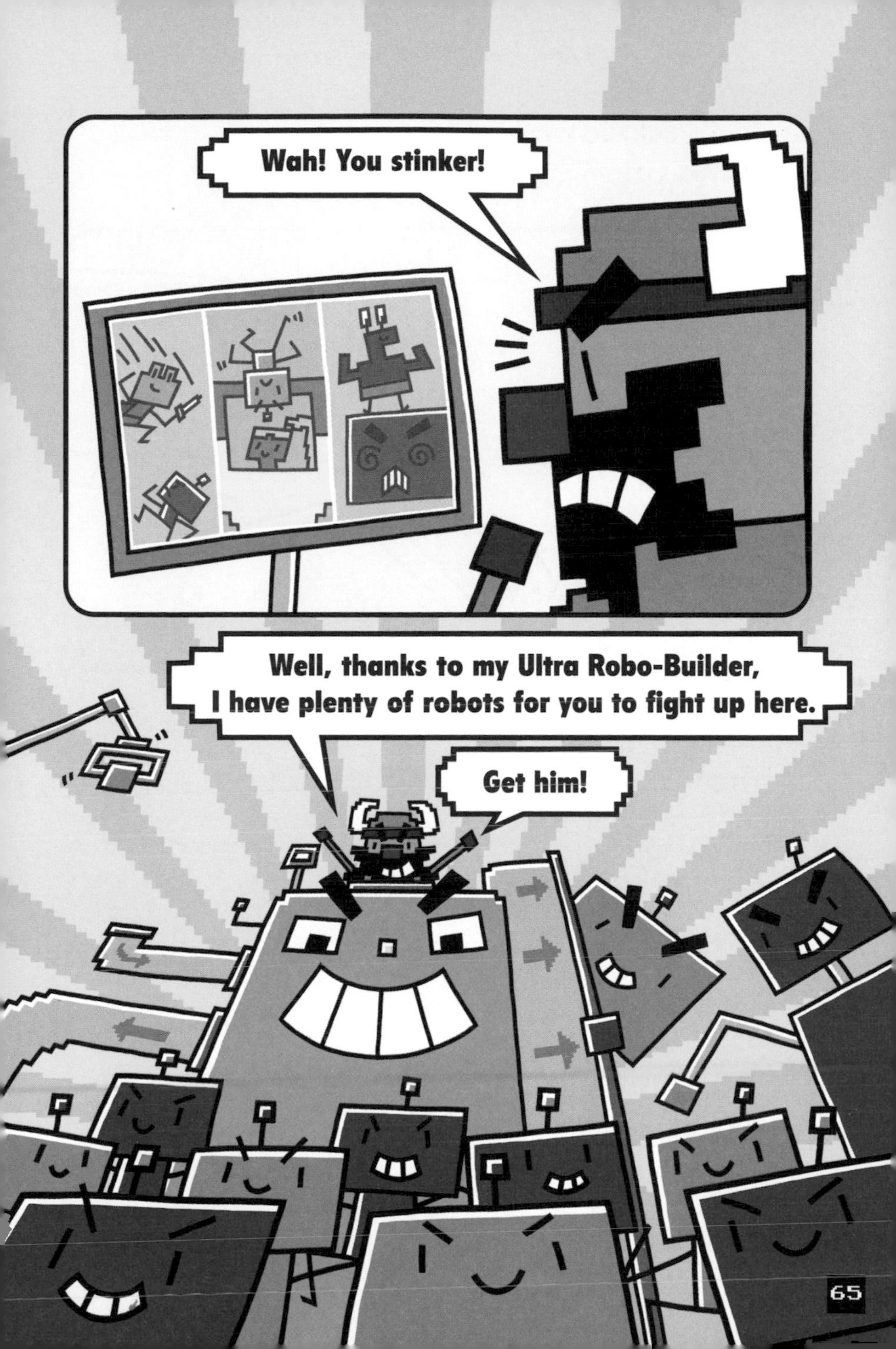
Wah! You stinker!
Well, thanks to my Ultra Robo-Builder,
I have plenty of robots for you to fight up here.
Get him!

All the robots in the room charge toward Super Rabbit Boy!

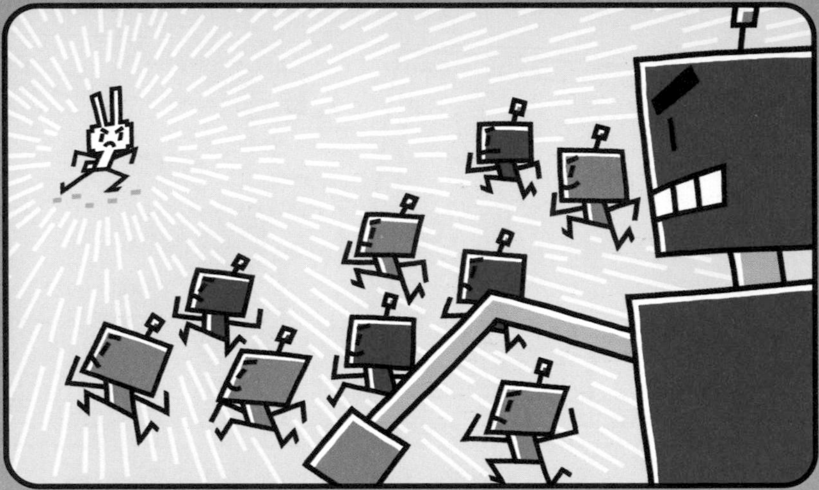

Super Rabbit Boy uses his Super Jump to bounce quickly from robot to robot.

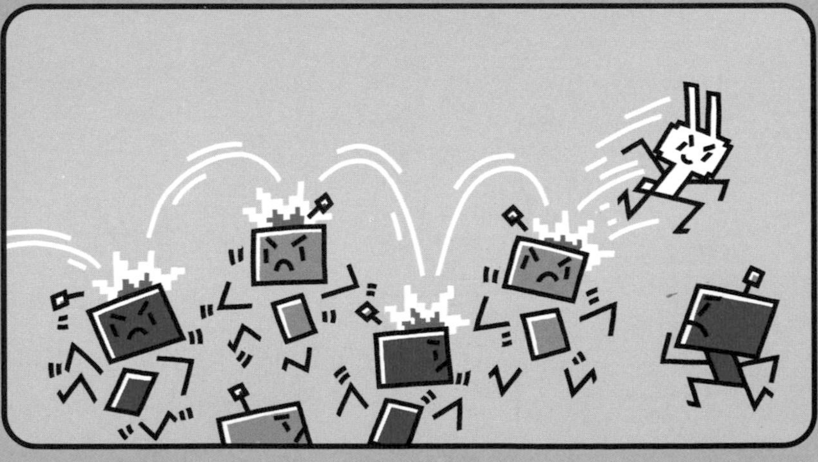

He easily destroys them all!

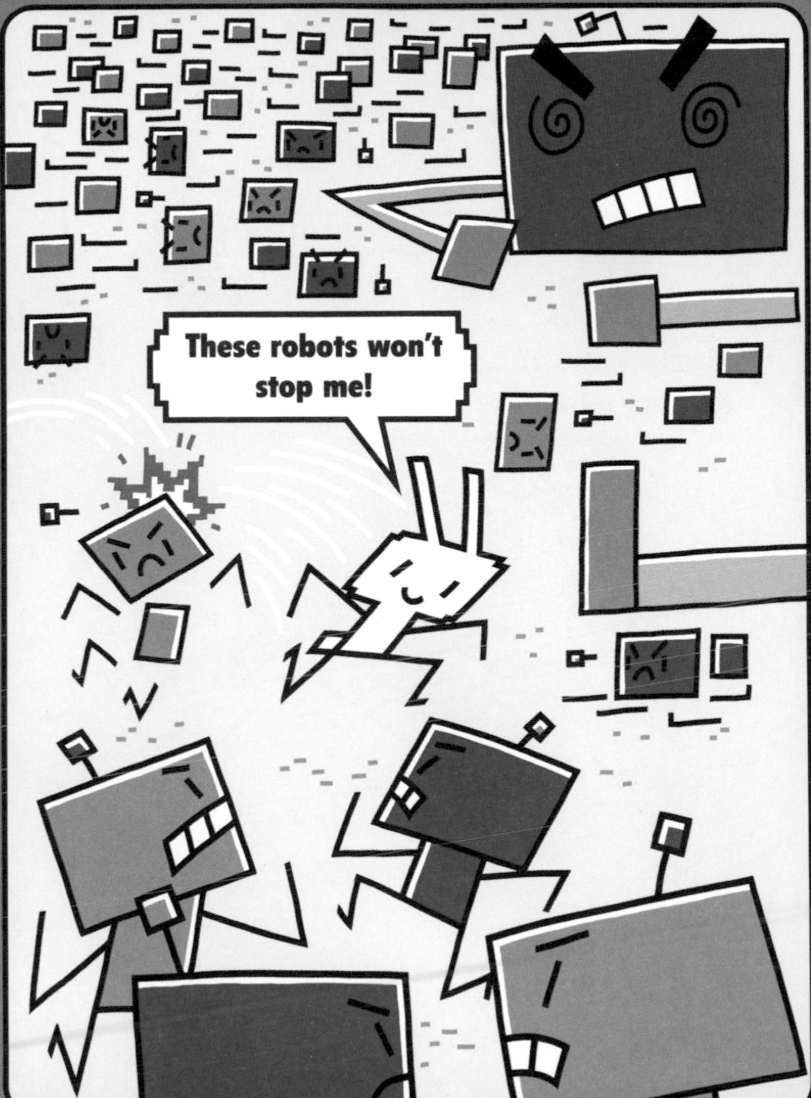
These robots won't stop me!

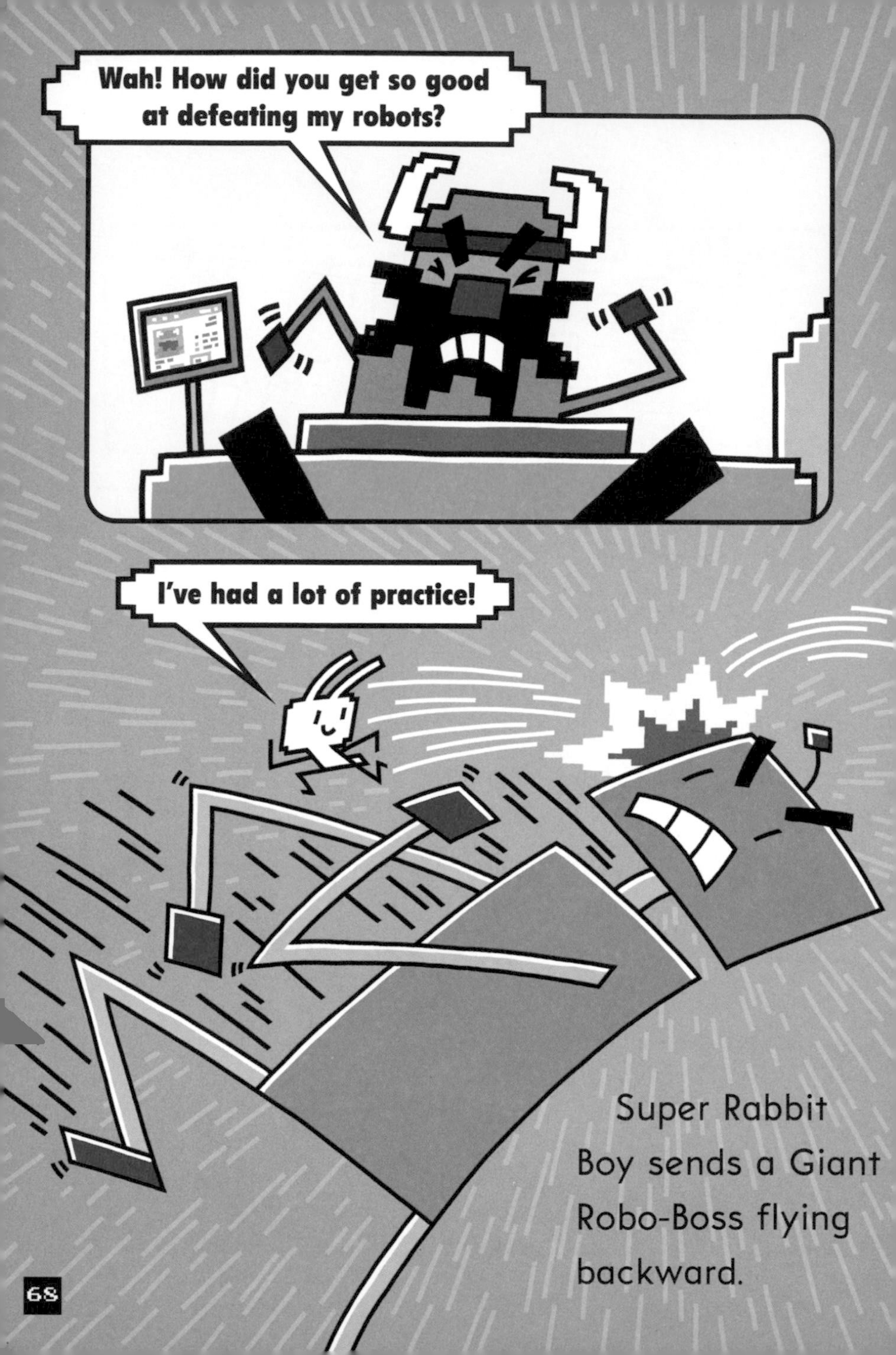
Wah! How did you get so good at defeating my robots?
I've had a lot of practice!

Super Rabbit Boy sends a Giant Robo-Boss flying backward.

The Giant Robo-Boss smashes into the Ultra Robo-Builder. The whole moon base starts to shake and shudder!

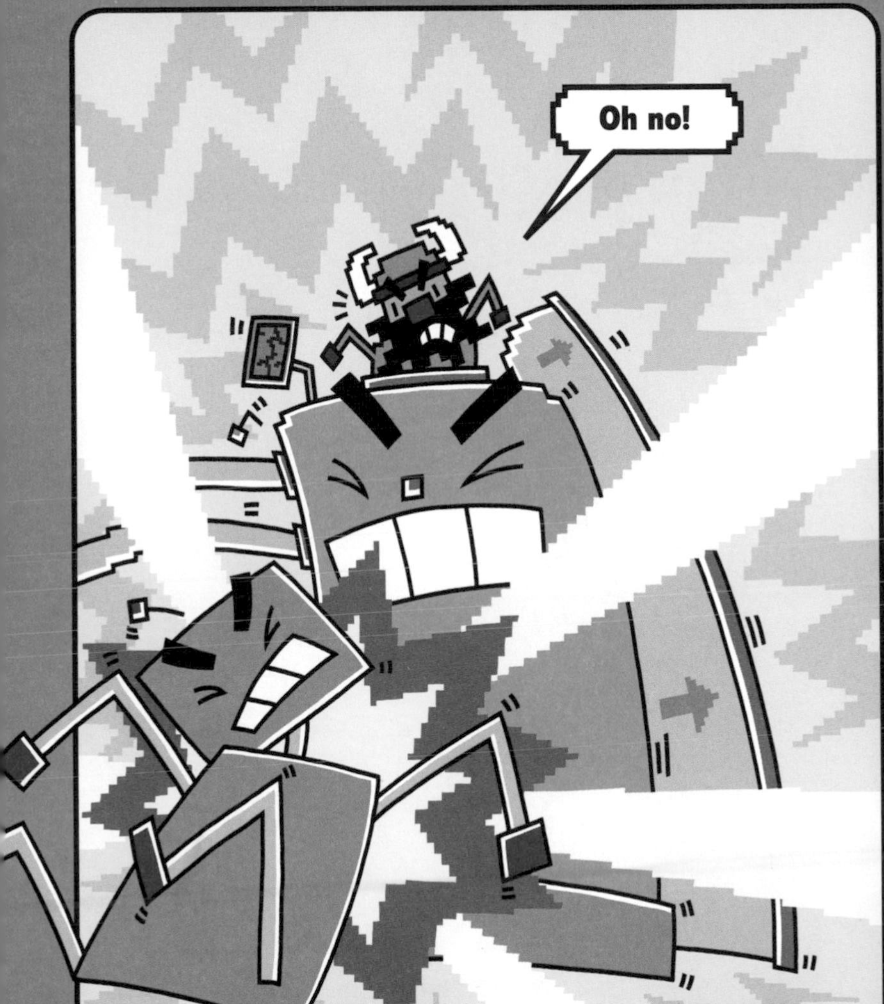
Oh no!

Super Rabbit Boy hops to safety. The moon base explodes with a big bang!

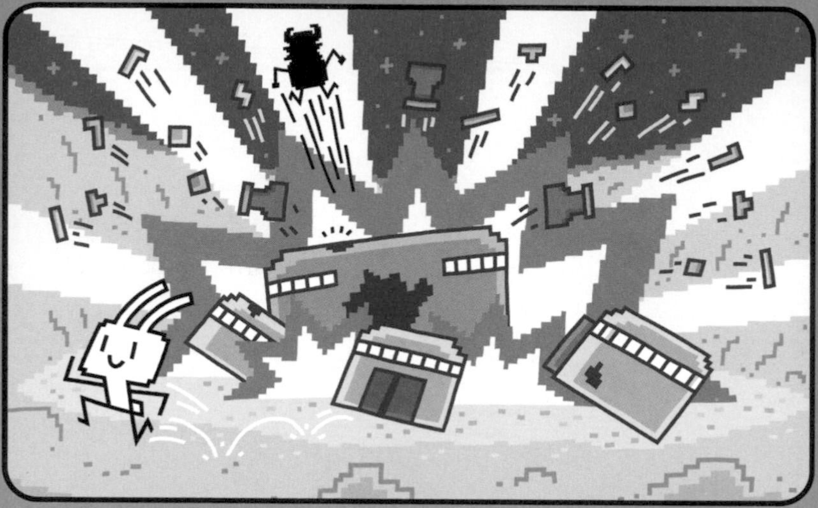

The explosion sends King Viking flying toward Super World.

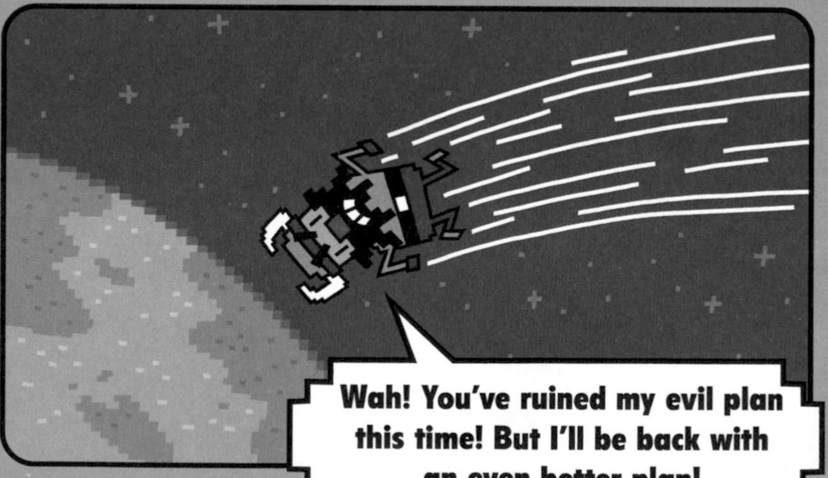
Wah! You've ruined my evil plan this time! But I'll be back with an even better plan!

Super Rabbit Boy heads back to Moon Girl's home. The other heroes are waiting there.

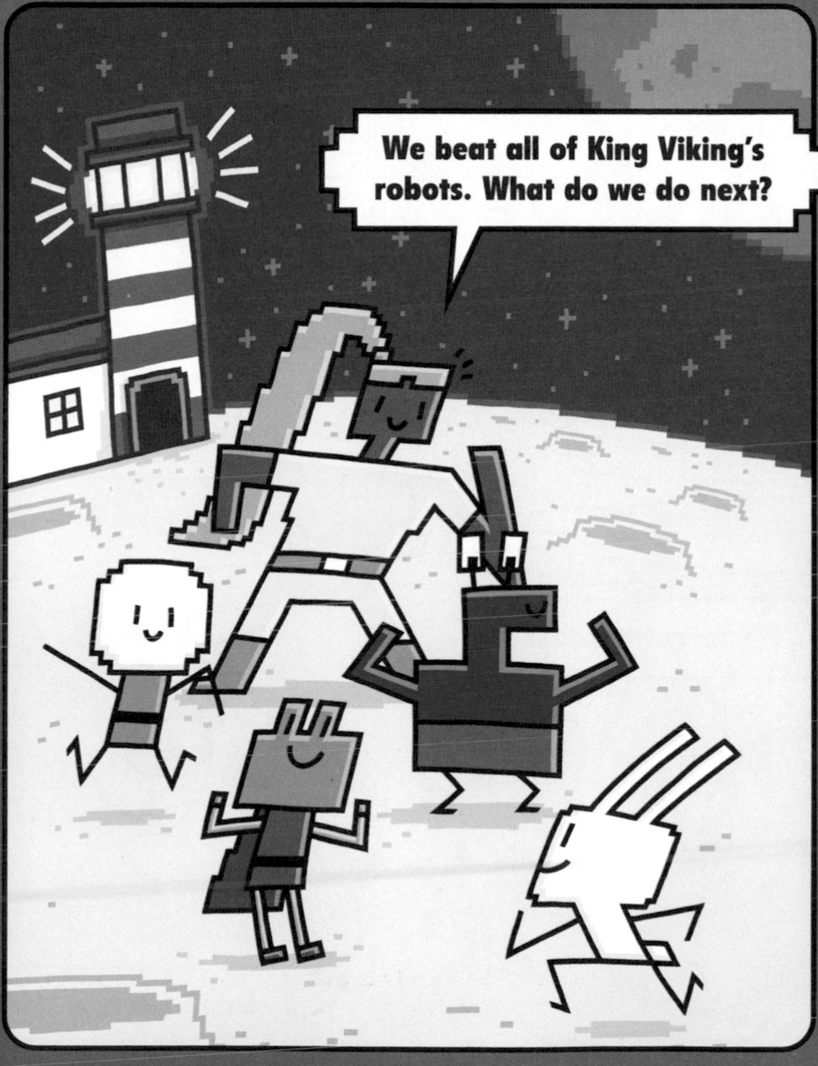
We beat all of King Viking's robots. What do we do next?

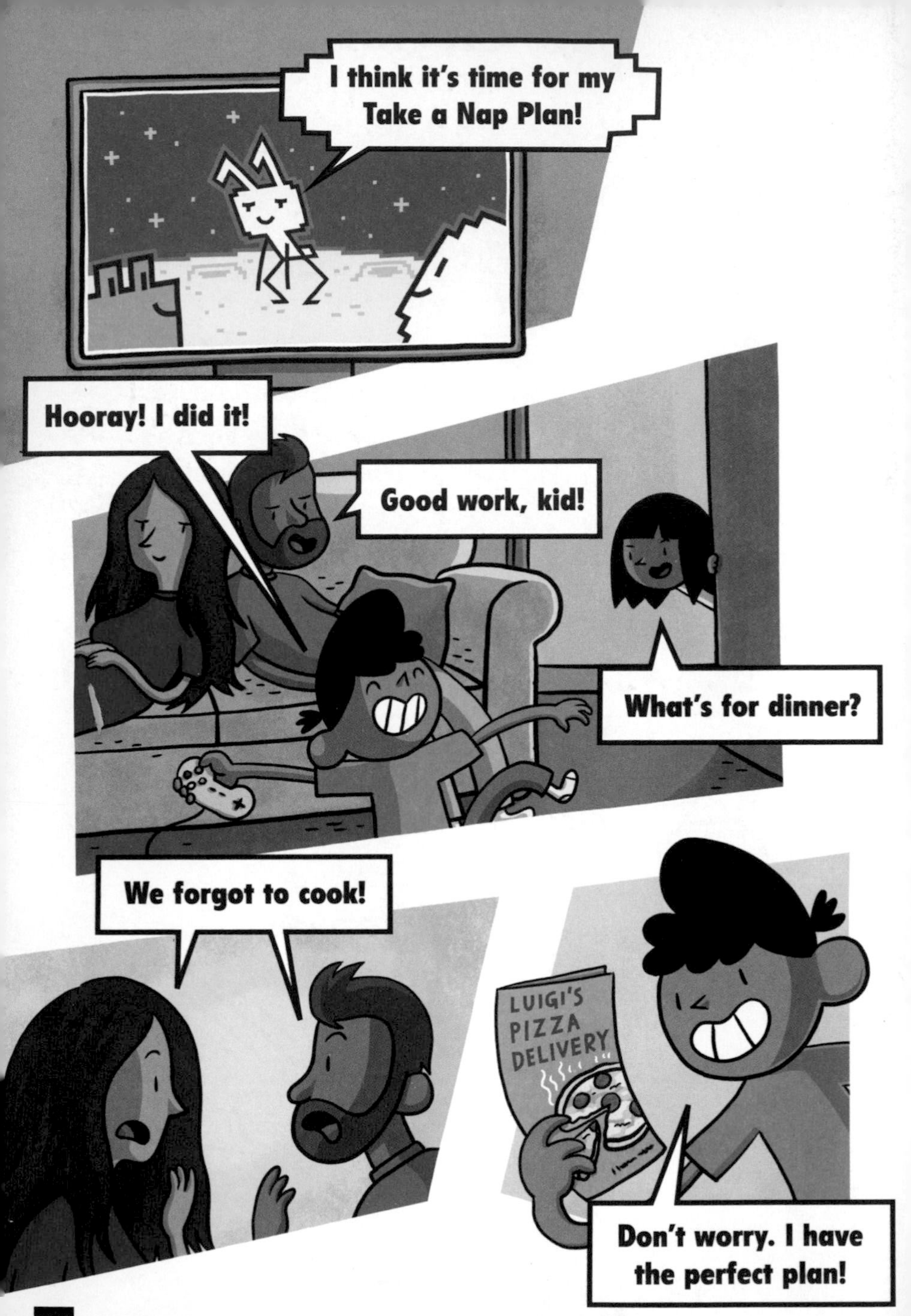
I think it's time for my Take a Nap Plan!
Hooray! I did it!
Good work, kid!
What's for dinner?
We forgot to cook!
LUIGI'S PIZZA DELIVERY
Don't worry. I have the perfect plan!

THOMAS FLINTHAM

has always loved to draw and tell stories, and now that is his job! He grew up in Lincoln, England, and studied illustration in Camberwell, London. He lives by the sea with his wife, Bethany, in Cornwall.

Thomas is the creator of THOMAS FLINTHAM'S BOOK OF MAZES AND PUZZLES and many other books for kids. PRESS START! is his first early chapter book series.

Moon Girl's friends — the Moon Mice — are not at home. Where could they have gone? Can you find three Moon Mice hiding elsewhere in this book?

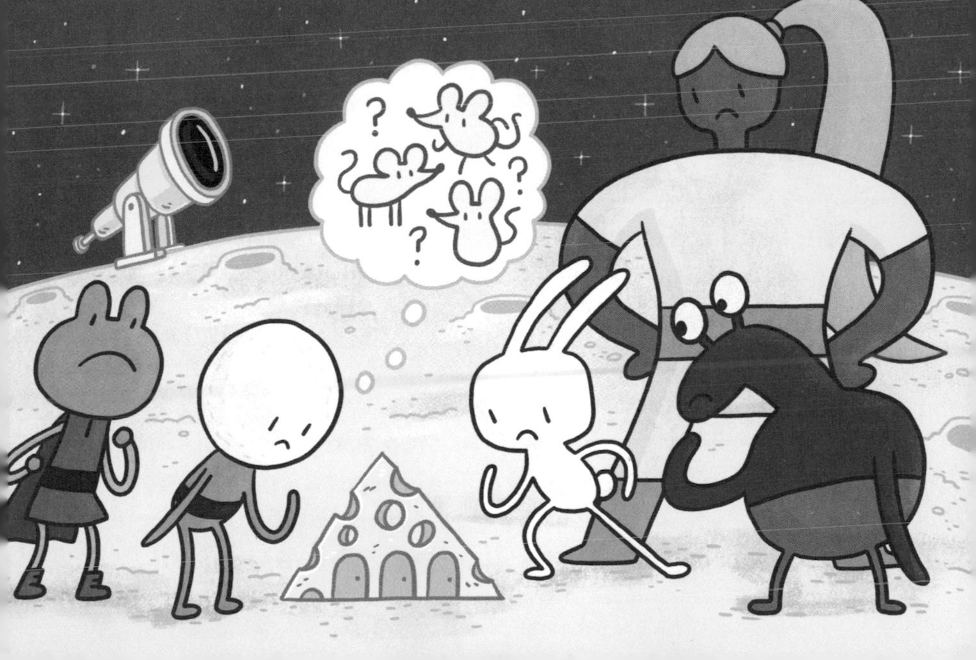

? ? ? ?

PRESS START!

How much do you know about SUPER RABBIT BOY WORLD!

Moon Girl uses a telescope to look down onto Super World from space. Read up on how telescopes work. How do they help you see things that are faraway?

What is the name of King Viking's evil plan? Why does he call it this?

In Chapter 7, Sunny has too much to do! How do his parents help him finish everything? And how does this experience help him win the game?

Where is King Viking while Super Rabbit Boy is busy fighting robots? How does Super Rabbit Boy finally find King Viking?

Super Rabbit Boy asks Frog Knight, Strong Girl, and Rogo to join his plan to stop King Viking. What does he call this plan? Imagine you and your friends make a plan to save the day. What is your plan called? Draw a diagram of your plan.